# HANNA
## MY
## HOLOCAUST
### STORY

**Scholastic Canada Ltd.**
604 King Street West, Toronto, Ontario M5V 1E1, Canada

**Scholastic Inc.**
557 Broadway, New York, NY 10012, USA

**Scholastic Australia Pty Limited**
PO Box 579, Gosford, NSW 2250, Australia

**Scholastic New Zealand Limited**
Private Bag 94407, Botany, Manukau 2163, New Zealand

**Scholastic Children's Books**
Euston House, 24 Eversholt Street, London NW1 1DB, UK

www.scholastic.ca

Library and Archives Canada Cataloguing in Publication
Alexander, Goldie, 1936-, author
Hanna / Goldie Alexander.

(My Holocaust story)
Originally published by Scholastic Australia, 2015.
Issued in print and electronic formats.
ISBN 978-1-4431-4813-9 (paperback).--ISBN 978-1-4431-4814-6 (html).--
ISBN 978-1-4431-4815-3 (Apple)

1. Holocaust, Jewish (1939-1945)--Juvenile fiction. I. Title.

PZ7.A3771Ha 2015          j823'.914          C2015-905475-3
                                             C2015-905476-1

First published by Scholastic Australia in 2015.
This edition published by Scholastic Canada Ltd. in 2016.

6 5 4 3 2 1      Printed in Canada  121   16 17 18  19  20

# HANNA
## MY
## HOLOCAUST
## STORY

**GOLDIE ALEXANDER**

Scholastic Canada Ltd.
Toronto New York London   Auckland Sydney
Mexico City New Delhi Hong Kong Buenos Aires

For David, and all extended family and descendents so they will always be aware of how lucky they are to be born in Australia.

# 1941

**W**e knew we were about to be killed. What we didn't understand was why it hadn't happened already. Where were these soldiers taking us?

Huddled in the rear of the German truck, we lurched over rough roads.

My brother Adam crouched on the floor. His eyes were closed. So were Mama's and Papa's. My little sister Ryzia kept up a constant whine.

As I nestled in beside them, my eyes stayed open.

Through a crack in the canvas, I could look outside as we sped to Otwock. The truck didn't stop. Instead we drove through the town and out the other side, pulling up in a birch forest.

It was so cold, the mist so thick, there was so much snow, I could just make out the silhouette of silvery tree trunks against a dismal grey sky.

The soldiers ordered us out of the truck. We were told to

line up. I closed my eyes and waited.

When nothing happened, I opened them again.

An SS officer, a member of Adolf Hitler's most loyal units, got out of the front cabin and strode toward us. He had the classic look of the German ideal Aryan: tall, slim, blond-haired, small-featured, pale blue eyes. His uniform was impeccable; the black belt around his tunic polished, his collar stiff, the silver insignia shining. Around his arm was the red armband bearing the symbol of the Nazis, the swastika. How I hated that crooked cross and what it represented.

The officer's ice-blue eyes regarded us as if we were rats, cockroaches or lice. In some way I couldn't blame him. We were painfully thin. Our clothes were in tatters. We looked just like the "degenerates" the Nazis called us. In the time we were hidden on the farm, Mama's hair had turned grey, and Papa's hair and stubble were quite white.

There would be no pity from that officer's gaze. It finally settled on my father.

He gave Papa the Nazi salute, keeping his right arm straight, raising it halfway, fingers pointed at the sky. "Romek Kaminsky?" His voice was soft, but cold.

Papa nodded.

The officer looked through some papers and said in German, "I have orders to bring you to Warsaw, to the Ghetto."

Papa stared in astonishment before replying in the same language. "Why?"

"It seems you are needed there."

We had left Warsaw two years ago. We had been hiding from the Nazis ever since in a farmhouse loft. Now it seemed as if it hadn't done us the least bit of good.

The truck drove into Warsaw, then through Aleje Jerozolimskie Street. I caught sight of "Kaminsky's Emporium," the business my family once owned. Though the building had survived the 1939 bombing raids, it looked terrible. All the store windows were covered by boards and every door bolted.

The truck continued along Nowy Swiat Street. As we went past our old house, Mama let out a faint cry. As if to taunt us, the buildings on either side were in ruins, yet our house was intact. The doorstep still edged onto the pavement. The brass door handle, that our housekeeper Elza used to polish so vigorously, still glittered.

I pictured my room with its low ceiling, carved blue headboard and quilted spread, my toys and books on their shelves in the wall opposite, the fringed rug on the polished wooden floor.

Who had been sleeping in my room? What had happened to all the furniture, paintings, books, rugs, silver, and crockery we had left behind? What about Mama's precious baby grand piano?

Angry blood rushed to my head.

Mama's eyes filled with tears. She'd been so houseproud, so happy with our home and her life as Papa's wife, someone loved and respected by all our relatives and friends.

We drove right through the city heading for the northern suburbs. A high concrete wall topped with broken glass and barbed wire was in front of us. The small entrance to what was behind the wall was heavily guarded. The German sentries waved us through.

We were in the ghetto. The streets were unbelievably crowded and everyone, it seemed, was Jewish. Everyone over the age of ten was branded with a blue Star of David either on a white armband or sewn onto their ragged clothing. Everyone was horribly thin, even thinner than we were, and their eyes were tired. Just like us, all these people had been forced by the Nazis to leave their homes and come here.

"What has happened to them, Papa?" I whispered.

Papa took my hand. "The ghetto is full of infection. Because of the cramped conditions, they're hard to avoid."

"What sort of illness?" Adam asked.

"Tuberculosis, a sickness of the lungs, is spread by coughing and sneezing. It will be everywhere here. Typhus too. It's carried by lice that burrow into your clothes and hair."

Mama held Ryzia closer. "Are there no medicines to cure them?"

"Yes, but they're expensive, and almost impossible to get

inside the ghetto." Papa sighed. "We must try not to brush against other people."

I think Papa believed we'd be dead before we had time to get sick. But in that case, why did the Nazis bother bringing us here? Why hadn't they shot us in the forest?

The truck lurched to a halt, flinging us against its canvas sides.

We heard the front door open.

The canvas at the back of the vehicle was pulled aside. Once my eyes adjusted to the light, I made out the shape of the tall SS officer.

"*Raus!* Out!" he yelled.

Frozen, lips chapped and sore, stiff from sitting in a cramped position for too long and bruised from being thrown around each time the truck cornered, we clambered onto the road.

I didn't dare glance at Papa. I was so frightened, the butterflies in my stomach refused to lie down. But I refused to show that officer how scared I was. I took a deep breath and tried to stand as if about to tackle a difficult vault in a gymnastic routine.

The officer pulled a sheet of paper out of an upper pocket. Handing it to Papa, he said, "Romek Kaminsky, you have been ordered to attend the Jewish Council as a translator."

Papa's chin dropped. "You mean—you brought me here to work?"

"A decree was issued last year establishing this ghetto. You are needed to process the Jews sent here." The officer gave my father such a disdainful look, Papa took an involuntary step back.

"But . . . but where are we to live?" Mama blurted.

"That is not my concern. The only command I've been given is to bring you here." He gave the Nazi salute, and with a "*Heil Hitler*," climbed back into the truck.

We stood there trembling. Partly from shock. Mostly with relief. We couldn't believe it. We were still alive.

"What do we do now?" Mama's voice was barely audible.

Papa was reading the official piece of paper the SS officer had handed him. He said, "Let's find this Jewish Council and see what they can do for us."

He stopped a passerby to ask him where to find it.

"You mean the Jewish Council of Elders?" the man answered, sarcastically. He spoke in Yiddish, the historical language of European Jews. "The Germans call it the *Judenrat*. However, I'm not sure if that council helps or hinders our people." He pointed to an imposing building a little further down the street. "Try the second floor." Tipping his hat to Mama, he continued down the street.

Papa, ever cautious, said, "This could be a trap. Best if I go there alone. Wait for me outside the building."

We squatted on the filthy pavement and leant against the wall.

As we sat there, I glanced up and saw three small boys head toward us. They weren't wearing stars, which meant they were less than ten years old. Every Jew older than ten was required by law to wear one. They were grubby and thin, their hair such a vermicelli tangle, their faces so pale, their eyes so shadowed, they made us look half normal.

The tallest looked directly at me. "You. Girl. Whatcha doing here?"

I cleared my throat, swallowed hard and managed, "We just came."

"What's your names?"

I stared at him suspiciously, before asking, "Why do you want to know?"

He stared back unabashed. "Just do!"

It probably wouldn't make any difference to tell him. "I'm Hanna. That's my mama, Adam, my brother, and my little sister Ryzia. She's three."

"How come you're wearing an armband?" He made this sound like an accusation. "You don't look old enough."

"Well, I am," I said wearily. "I'm twelve."

His mouth curled in disbelief. "You're real short. I think you're only eight or nine."

I was too exhausted to bother with this cheeky brat. "I can't help being short," I snapped. "You're not so big yourself."

"Where you from?" he fired back.

How much should I tell them? But what could they do to us that hadn't happened already?

I said, "We were living on a farm outside Otwock." I thought of Elza and Anya, who had hidden us since the war began in 1939.

"So if you were on a farm, how come you're here?"

"A neighbour turned us in. The people that hid us were shot." Tears started to build in the corner of my eyes. Before they could fall, I glared up at him. "So, who are you?"

"Me, I'm Karol." He pointed a filthy finger at his friends. "Those two, Jacob and Moshe. We're a gang."

I sniffed in disbelief. Before the war Adam and his best friend Alex always talked about being a gang. As if this boy suspected I wasn't taking him seriously, he said, "We trade with the Poles and sell back to the Jews, sometimes the other way around."

I didn't get to hear more, because just then Papa came out of the building, cheeks flushed with excitement. "Come," he told Mama. "We have been lucky. They have given me work! So I will earn a few zlotys. Best of all, we have somewhere to live."

I got to my feet and helped Mama onto hers. She looked so spent, I took Ryzia from her, and the little one snuggled into my shoulder. When I next looked around, Karol and his friends had vanished into the crowd.

We set off through the streets, passing bundles of rags on the pavement. Only they weren't rags, they were people curled up in balls or leaning against walls.

Many held out a hand begging for food. Why didn't they have food? Didn't they have any money? Wasn't there any food to buy? A little girl, she could have been no more than three years old, looked at us with giant eyes. "Please," she murmured. I felt terrible for her but there was nothing I could do.

Papa led us around the corner along a number of streets until we arrived at Zelazna Street. Here, he kept going until we arrived at a triple-storey house. Maybe once the building had been handsome, but now the facade was cracked, the glass in the windows wore crazy zigzag lines, and the concrete steps leading to the front door seemed ready to collapse.

Papa said, "We are fortunate. The ghetto is so crowded, it's almost impossible to find somewhere to live. Many people have to survive on the streets. But because I am now employed as a translator, we can use two rooms on the second floor. They have even given me money so we can buy food."

Papa took a key out of his pocket and opened the front door. We walked into a narrow passage. Immediately, we were hit by the stink of boiled cabbage, damp and urine. It felt even colder inside than out.

In the corridor a door opened. A woman peered out. Her face was old and wrinkled but her hair was thick and black. It took me a moment to realize she was wearing a *sheitel*, a wig. That told me she was an Orthodox Jew. Papa handed her a piece of paper. She read it through very slowly, grunted and gave him a grudging smile. "Up there," she told him. "First floor, praise *HaShem* . . . praise God. Your rooms are at the front." She went back inside slamming the door behind her.

The rooms were empty, apart from a chamber pot. The floorboards were as bare as the dirty walls.

Papa picked up the chamber pot and placed it in the passage.

I never thought I could miss our cramped hiding space in the farm loft. But I did.

Mama settled Ryzia on the floor and lay down next to her, curling her body around the toddler in an attempt to share warmth and comfort.

Papa stared through the murky glass in the window. "I'll see if I can find us food and blankets."

I struggled onto my feet. "Can I come? I'll help carry them."

Papa considered it. "Yes, Hanna, you're to come with me.

Adam, you're to stay here and look after Mama and Ryzia."

Adam nodded at Papa and, holding his left arm up from the elbow, he waggled his right fist across it. He was playing his imaginary violin, something he did all the time.

Back on the street, I said, "Papa, where do we go?"

"I'm told there's a market close by. Tomorrow I will return to buy furniture. I have enough money to make us more comfortable."

I followed him. We went down Zielna Street and then made several turns, all the time forced to dodge people flocking along the pavements. All the Jews, a third of the original population of Warsaw, had been sent to this tiny area in the city. Others had been sent here from the provinces.

A car bearing the Nazi flag drove past almost running over several men. Though they jumped aside just in time, their bodies moved heavily and slowly.

"That car must belong to Jozef Szerynski," Papa said, "a Jew who has turned against us. He's in charge of the Jewish Police Force."

"A *Jewish* police force." My eyebrows shot up. "Why do we need that?"

"Given the conditions we have been left with, I suppose the Germans are hoping we'll kill each other and save them the trouble."

"Do they have to wear uniforms?"

"No, but they have their own armband, to identify them.

They also carry a rubber club attached to their belts and are given a bigger food ration. Seems," Papa dryly added, "they have total permission to order us around."

By then we had arrived at the market. Everywhere I looked, people were selling and buying food, clothing, furniture, paintings, crockery, silverware and goodness knows what else. It seemed as if anything and everything was for sale.

Papa bought a small loaf of rye bread, a wedge of cheese, a pickled herring, a jar of fat, a small quantity of black sump oil, and sweets that tasted like sugar but turned out to be mostly molasses and saccharin.

We also needed blankets. We only had the clothes we wore. Though it was early spring, there was still snow on the ground and it was desperately cold.

Papa strode toward a man holding up a blanket. I galloped after him.

Papa examined the blankets before looking at the man selling them. He gave an astonished cry. "Isaac?"

Pan Isaac, an old friend of Papa's, had once been a respected and wealthy banker. He took a few moments to recognize my father, they had both changed so much.

"Romek, my friend . . ." Tears dripped into Isaac's beard. "That we have come to this."

"Yes," Papa said with a sigh. He remained silent a moment, as if he knew no words that could express what he was feeling. Then he remembered why we were here. "How much do you want for those blankets?"

"My friend, what can you give me? My wife and children, we have no food. Nothing to eat . . . nothing. I am selling what little we have left."

"I can give you all I have," said Papa emptying his pockets.

"That's too much," Pan Isaac protested. "You must keep these zlotys for another day."

But Papa pressed the money into his old friend's hand saying, "I am to be employed by the Jewish Council and they will pay me enough to keep us alive."

Isaac embraced Papa and both men wept.

I watched the men silently crying. I remembered Papa and Pan Isaac together, as the men they used to be, two years previously, the day the war began . . .

# 1939

Our building edged onto a busy street. It was one of Warsaw's historic thoroughfares, full of shops, restaurants and fine houses. In the rattle of passing cars, trams, horses and carts, no one heard me come in. I was upset about missing my regular gymnastic class because of a sore throat and blocked nose. I had never missed a class before.

Passing the door to Papa's study, I heard the unmistakeable sound of an argument. I recognized my father's voice and that of his friend, Pan Isaac. I knew Zaida, my grandfather, was home too, because his ebony-handled umbrella was in the hallstand and he never went out without it.

"You think," Papa was shouting, "that we are safe?"

My father wasn't usually home on a Tuesday afternoon. For several generations our family had been the proud owners of Kaminskys' Emporium in the heart of the city, and Papa spent long days there. He claimed that we mightn't own the biggest clothing store in Warsaw, but it was certainly the best.

Pan Isaac said something that I couldn't hear, other than the word "*Kristallnacht*." I froze. *Kristallnacht*, "crystal night"—the night of the broken glass—was the name given to the night in November last year when Jewish people and their businesses, hospitals, schools and synagogues were attacked in Germany and Austria. It wasn't only Nazi soldiers that did it. Ordinary people had joined in too. Even though Mama and Papa had tried to prevent me and Adam hearing too much about it on the radio, or seeing photographs in the newspapers, I knew enough for the word to send shivers through me.

I knelt close to the keyhole and listened more carefully.

"Look at what's happened in Berlin!" Papa still sounded furious. "Tens of thousands of Jews were arrested. What makes you think it won't be the same here?"

Zaida's voice rose. "But Romek, a third of this city is Jewish." I pictured his goatee beard waggling, his eyeglass falling onto his waistcoat like it always does when he's upset. "There's no way they can put a third of the city in prison."

"No?" Papa still sounded angry. "Don't be so sure. The Nazis are noted for their efficiency."

"So! What should we do?"

"I kept telling you we should have left. Now it's probably too late. At least we should be sending money to Switzerland."

"I think that would be wise," said Pan Isaac. Until recently he had been a successful banker. But the bans against Jews in

Germany had affected his bank as well, and he was no longer allowed to work there.

"Right now we need all our money to bring in more stock," Zaida insisted.

"Maybe." A long pause before Papa added, "Still, as a precaution, I think we must hide money somewhere in this house."

"I'm sure that isn't necessary," Zaida said crossly.

"The German army has already taken over Austria, and parts of the Czechoslovak Republic," Pan Isaac reminded him. "Germany has made it clear that Poland will be next. There are people in the streets demonstrating against Germany's plans."

"But Britain and France are friends of Poland. They have promised to defend us if we should need it," Zaida insisted. "Surely, that will stop Hitler."

"Maybe. Maybe not. And without their help, our cavalry will never stand up to the Nazi's armoured tanks."

Lately, the streets of Warsaw had been filled with uniformed soldiers wearing flowing capes and polished knee-high boots. They were so handsome that Adam, my seven-year-old brother, dreamt one day of joining the Polish cavalry.

I strained to hear more through the keyhole, but the men's voices had died down to a murmur.

Instead, I went into the kitchen where I found Mama and

Elza preparing supper. Even with my blocked nose I could smell chocolate, cinnamon and other spices.

My baby sister Ryzia was on the floor playing with her favourite teddy bear. Mama looked up as I came in. "Hannale, why are you home this early? Don't you have a gymnastic class?"

I pulled out a hankie and blew my nose. "Panna Margrete said my cold was too bad, so she sent me home."

"Drink some tea, and help yourself to some cake. That might make you feel better," Mama suggested. "And there is a parcel on the table for you. It's from Nanna Goldberg."

I had turned eleven the week before, so I knew it must be my birthday present. Mama's parents, the Goldbergs, had moved to Paris three years ago. They always sent me wonderful presents: perfume, silk scarves and lots of books.

I didn't miss Mama's parents all that much. Nanna Goldberg was amazingly critical. She never approved of Mama not employing a German governess to teach us "language and proper behaviour." Nanna thought everything German was "high class"—their language, culture, literature, music—and she looked down on everything else. When I asked Mama why her parents hadn't gone to Berlin where Nanna might surely have been happier, she told me her father did most of his business with France. He bought hats from famous designers and sold them on to the wealthy women of Warsaw.

I opened the present. There were three books and some soft, grey leather gloves. I held them against my cheek as I looked at the books. They were in French, a language I didn't study. I was surprised they weren't in German.

As much as I loved the gloves, and Elza's chocolate and cinnamon babka, they were a poor consolation for missing my class. I loved gymnastics. I'd mastered sprinting down a runway, vaulting from a springboard over a wooden horse, and landing on both feet with arms raised. On the beam, I could run, skip and do forward and backward circles. Hanging from a bar with both hands, then only one, I could swing into different positions and loop over the bar. On the mat, I was able to manage complicated somersaults and spins.

Panna Margrete, my gymnastic teacher, often said, "Hanna, you have the ideal proportions for a gymnast. With more practice you will be good enough to enter some competitions." I was still only four-feet-nine and weighed eighty-five pounds. I looked a lot like Mama, though she was four inches taller. Our faces were upside-down triangles: we both had wide cheekbones and pointy chins, full lips, and dark hair. I really hated my hair as I could never coax it into a proper pageboy style, no matter how much I brushed it.

Papa was tall and stout, with thick, strong dark-brown hair that sprang from his scalp like it had a life all its own, the same hair I inherited. He had charcoal eyes, a strong nose, full lips, and a bristly moustache that prickled when he kissed me. Like Zaida, he was always impeccably turned out. He'd say, "How can I sell Kaminskys' clothes, if I'm not equally well dressed?"

My brother Adam was tall for seven and promised to be quite handsome when he grew up. He had fairer hair than the rest of us, hazel eyes and small features. Right now he was quite thin, but he was strong and wiry . . . I knew how strong he was because whenever we wrestled it was hard to beat him.

Ryzia was only ten months old and she took after Papa. She had the same thick dark hair, dark eyes, chubby pink cheeks, a dimpled chin, and a rosebud mouth.

Right now she was holding out her arms to be picked up.

I did and settled her on my hip.

Mama and Elza were cooking chicken soup with dumplings. As I watched Elza stir the pot, my mouth watered at the heavenly smell.

Elza was our housekeeper. Taller and sturdier than Mama, with a mole on her right cheek like a squashed raisin, she thought nothing of doing a hard day's cleaning, washing, helping Mama prepare dinner, and then spending hours playing with us. I loved the way the skin around her pale blue eyes crinkled when she gave us her abrupt laugh. Mama was very fond of her. I think their friendship was unusual, as other families we knew frequently changed housekeepers.

I had known Elza since I was a baby. I knew she regarded

us children almost as her own and would do anything in her power to protect us. She was the best person I knew. A real mensch.

Elza grew up in a farm not far from Otwock, twenty-four kilometres southeast of Warsaw, where she had to feed the cows, pigs and chickens, carry buckets of water and firewood into the house, and help out in the fields. No wonder she ran away. I think her parents had been unkind to her, because she often said, her eyes watering with emotion, "You Kaminskys are my family now."

Before we left for upstairs, Elza slipped me two homemade cookies. Clutching the biscuits and with Ryzia on my hip, I set off, Mama calling after us, "Don't get the baby too excited. It's almost time for her bath and supper."

Like many three-storey buildings in Nowy Swiat Street, ours had a cellar where we stored anything we didn't use. At the front of the house was Papa's study, the dining room and parlour with its armchairs, sofas, small and large tables. An elaborately carved silver samovar sat on the largest dresser. This samovar was only used when Mama held an "English" afternoon tea where the most delicate sandwiches and delicious cakes were served. Me and Adam always looked forward to these as we got all the leftovers. When grown-ups drank tea brewed in that samovar, it was usually served weak and black, sipped with a cube of sugar or with a cherry or strawberry jam called varenyi.

In the furthest corner sat a baby grand piano. Though I took weekly lessons from Pan Schmidt, I was no natural musician. However, Mama performed well enough to give small recitals, and Adam had only to hear a melody to play it on his violin. Pan Schmidt claimed he was a "child prodigy."

We each had our own bedroom. Plus there were two bathrooms: one for Papa and Mama, the other for the rest of the family. Right at the back of the house was the kitchen and laundry. Behind the laundry was the small room where Elza slept.

I peered into Adam's room. He was on his bed reading and didn't see me. He had stayed home from school with a cold, which he'd obviously gifted to me. Then I took Ryzia into hers. We had just settled on the floor with her wooden blocks when I heard a loud thud, then another, then another, each louder than the last.

My heart leapt into my mouth. My heart thumped against my ribs.

It took me a long moment to realize what was happening.
Bombs!
Warsaw was being bombed.
Sirens began to wail.

There was so much noise, I trembled and Ryzia burst into tears. As I tried to soothe her, Mama raced up the stairs calling for us to run down to the cellar. Papa, Zaida and Pan Isaac followed us. We could smell the smoke filling the streets. "Hurry! Hurry!" Papa urged.

Most Warsaw houses were built to withstand the long, cold, dark winters. Roofs were steeply pitched so snow could easily slide off, and there was often a crane to help lift heavy furniture to upper floors. Windows were small, set inside thick triple-brick walls, surrounded by embrasures, and double-glazed. One window swung in, one swung out; this to keep out the intense cold of winter. Each apartment had its own metal cast-iron heaters fuelled with coal or coke, and covered in polished tiles. The wealthier the house, the more elaborate these were. Floors consisted of wide strips of polished blond wood covered with patterned rugs and carpets to provide extra warmth.

Every street corner in Warsaw had a café where writers, musicians and artists used to meet because many of them could only afford to live in tiny, badly heated rooms.

Crouched in the cellar, I thought of our beautiful city and what must be happening to it. When I couldn't bear to think this way anymore, I closed my eyes and clutched Zaida's hands. Zaida had come to live with us when my bubba, his wife, died. Whenever I was in trouble, or hurt myself, he was always the first to comfort me. He was never shy about showing how much he loved his grandchildren.

Only this afternoon Papa had been warning Zaida of the German threat to Poland. Now the Luftwaffe's bombs had succeeded in convincing us that all was about to change.

Next morning I asked Mama if I could go to my best friend Eva Lublinski's house. I was worried that she and her family might be hurt. Mama had tried phoning them, but the line was dead.

Mama shook her head. "It's not safe. I can't let you wander the streets, or even go to school. Not until we know what is happening. I don't want to let you, or Adam and Ryzia, out of my sight."

Over the next few days we spent a lot of time in the cellar. It was early September and, thankfully, still quite warm. We filled wooden boxes with tins of food, bottles of water, candles, and other essentials. I took some of my favourite books and a pack of cards. Whenever things got me down I played Patience. One of Grandma Goldberg's presents was a tiny pack of cards that fitted inside my pocket. Concentrating on a game helped me stay calm.

Mama and Papa and Zaida talked together in hushed voices about what they thought was happening. As I wanted to know, I listened as hard as I could. Mama kept saying, "We should have gone to my parents' in Paris."

Papa shrugged, "Too late now."

Just as they promised, Britain and France declared war on Germany in response to the Nazis' invasion of Poland. Hearing this came as a relief. Britain and France had helped to defeat Germany in the last war, twenty years ago. Maybe that would happen again?

"Germany is a different country now though," Papa warned. "Hitler has been building up his forces for years. And the German people's devotion to him is beyond measure. We've all seen the way millions turn out to his rallies and just to see him in the streets. But the Nazis aren't an army plucked from the people at the last moment like ours. They're highly trained professionals.

"I still find it hard to understand why those Berlin Jews admired Hitler's new order," Papa went on. "Didn't they listen to what he was saying? It took *Kristallnacht* for this to really sink in. Shops smashed, people attacked and deported to prison camps. The Nazis made no pretence as to what they hoped to achieve."

Though Zaida couldn't argue with this, he kept insisting, "In the end they can't win. The final triumph must always go to a just cause."

When the planes came at night we stayed awake listening to them circle the skies above our city.

"Why do they fly around like that?" Adam asked.

"They're getting their bearings," he explained.

Then the bombs began to drop.

Things began to get worse. And quickly. The only way we knew what was going on was from what we heard over the wireless. These broadcasts informed us that German armoured units had reached Wola, an area in the west of the city, and that the Polish navy, which had been anchored at Gdynia, had taken refuge at a British naval base.

Papa was told he had to join the Polish forces for compulsory military training in the east. All able-bodied men were conscripted to try to keep the Germans out. Papa had to leave without delay. Over one hundred thousand Polish soldiers were ready to defend our city.

We listened to the wireless almost non-stop. We cheered when we heard our army had stopped the German advance. We were so thrilled—and so proud of Papa, fighting to protect Poland.

Then the news changed. Our city was under siege. The Germans were surrounding Warsaw.

We spent days and nights in the cellar. The air raids and the shelling from heavy artillery guns didn't stop. We could hear high-pitched bursts of gunfire repeating in the distance: "Ack-ack-ack-ack-ack, ack-ack-ack-ack-aack."

I asked, "What's that sound, Mama?"

"Anti-aircraft guns," Adam answered for her.

Elza fretted about food. She insisted on leaving the cellar

to get provisions from the kitchen.

"No, Elza," Mama protested. "It's just not safe."

"It's no use sitting here to slowly starve," Elza argued. "I'd rather take the risk of a bomb falling on my head."

"Let me go, Mama," I begged. "I'm quick."

Mama shook her head very fiercely.

"No," Elza declared. "It's my job to look after you, and I won't let a few Nazis let us go hungry." Without another word, she disappeared up the cellar steps.

She returned soon after carrying some bread and cheese. "There's dust and ash everywhere," she reported. "But otherwise nothing a broom won't fix."

I wasn't sure if our neighbours had been as lucky.

After the bombing didn't let up for more than a week, Elza insisted that she must go to check the state of the city.

The wait for her to come back seemed endless. It was only an hour or so, but as every minute ticked by, we hoped and prayed she was safe. We could hear planes droning overhead and bombs falling.

Just as we were starting to lose hope, she emerged at the top of the stairs. Her face was grim as she reported what she'd seen. "There's piles of rubble everywhere, buildings gone, and worse. Two houses at the end of northern end have gone, and the houses on either side of us are damaged."

"Oh, no," Mama cried. "The Balinskis?"

Elza nodded sadly. "I saw young Dominik. The family are

all right, they are staying with Mr. Balinski's sister. Dominik and his father are working as volunteers, putting out fires. They are desperate for help."

"I could do that, Mama!" Adam cried.

"No," Mama said firmly. "You're too young."

Adam looked disappointed.

A few days later Elza ventured out again. We had almost run out of water and the taps no longer worked. I don't know what we could have done without Elza. She had become our lifeline.

She returned holding a half full bucket and saying, "This is all I could find. Then she grimly added, "The Nazis have destroyed all the waterworks."

"Then we will have to make do," I said decisively. "Won't we, Mama?"

Mama didn't answer. But Zaida did. "Yes, we will."

The fighting went on throughout September. On the 28th, the word spread that Poland had surrendered. We had no idea what would happen next, or where Papa was. Three days later, there was an urgent knock on the door.

"I'll go," Zaida said.

As the door opened we saw Papa—his face grey with

exhaustion, his hat, coat and boots covered in grime, but he was all in one piece. We were so relieved to see him, we couldn't stop crying. Even Zaida's tears ran into his beard.

Papa looked at us amazed, then said, "Don't tell me you're crying because I came home?"

We couldn't stop hugging him.

"What happened to you?" Mama cried.

"Yes," Zaida echoed. "Tell us everything."

Papa sank onto a chair and looked around as if he couldn't believe where he was. "The German army surrounded the city," Papa explained. "The Luftwaffe bombarded not just us, but strategic targets—barracks, factories, hospitals. They got the waterworks too."

We all nodded. "Elza told us," Mama said.

"We fought the best we could, but the Polish army was hopelessly outnumbered. And the Russian army was advancing from the east. We didn't stand a chance, especially given the state of the city, and we knew it. We would have to surrender. Once we realized this, we started to hide some of our weapons and ammunition. Maybe we will get a chance to use them to fight back again. I hope so."

"But we heard that most of the Army has been taken prisoner. How did you escape?" Mama wanted to know.

Papa smiled grimly. "Hiding behind a bombed-out building. I waited a long time before I dared think it safe to come home."

"Thank God," Mama whispered. "We thought we'd never see you again."

After the surrender, things seemed to quieten down. Mama insisted I go back to school. Luckily my school had survived the siege. Others hadn't. I was anxious to see my friends, Eva in particular.

We'd been best friends ever since we met on our first day there. Eva was slim and a full head taller than me. She had straight blonde hair, blue-green eyes and small features. She didn't look the least bit Jewish. I knew some of the boys in our class really liked her, because they did stupid things, like toss pencils and erasers at her, and show off in the playground when they thought she might be watching.

She never took any notice. "Those idiots!" she'd say and we'd walk to some place where they couldn't bother us.

Both Eva and I were good students. Eva was better at arithmetic, geometry and algebra, while my favourite subjects were geography, history, Polish, and of all things, German. Papa and Mama spoke German when they didn't want me to understand, but I had picked up enough to know what they were saying.

We both loved books. When we were young, Eva's

favourite was *Alice's Adventures in Wonderland*, even though the book was originally written in English. I preferred *Grimm's Fairy Tales*. As we got older I looked for books about history, books like *Ben Hur*. When war broke out, Eva was halfway through *David Copperfield*.

Going to school and being with Eva again made everything feel almost normal.

The Germans and the Russians took over Poland, dividing it between them. Our beautiful country was now occupied by not one, but two enemy armies.

The Nazi-appointed Governor General, Hans Frank, issued a decree that all Jewish men, women and children over ten had to wear a white armband with a blue Star of David on it to identify them.

I went looking for Zaida to ask, "Why? Are other people getting them too? Will Christians have to wear crosses?"

He shook his head. "No, just us. We are being singled out. We're no longer allowed to use public transport, go to cinemas and cafés, or you even to school." He sighed heavily and I caught a whiff of his cologne. He said, "They have told the Polish people to avoid Jewish-owned shops. That means our customers won't be able to buy from us anymore."

I turned to Papa. "I don't understand. What did we do wrong?"

Papa shrugged. "Nothing, *bubbala*." This was his pet name for me. "You have to understand that for centuries bad governments have blamed certain groups of people for their problems. They use them as scapegoats."

I still couldn't understand it. We were no different to anyone else. Why blame Jews for Germany's financial troubles? Even I knew that losing the Great War, ten years before I was born, had made life difficult for the Germans. But it was hardly our fault.

Papa said, "It's a standard political ploy to create a common enemy. Making people afraid of others helps keep a government in power. The government becomes the protector from the imagined threat, and that way it becomes even more powerful as people put their trust in them. That is what Herr Hitler is doing."

"I don't mind missing school." Adam sounded quite cheerful. "But why do they want to take away our wireless? They must have lots of radios already. Why can't we keep ours?"

Since the invasion, I rarely saw either of my parent's face soften into a smile. But now Papa managed a tiny one. "We are lucky in that we own two. That's why I hid the smaller one at the back of the cellar."

Unlike Adam, I was very upset about not being allowed to go to school. "I was doing well," I wailed. "And now I'll be behind in all my subjects. Other kids will still go, it's so unfair."

"Don't be so sure." Papa gave me a quick hug. "No children above grade four will be there. All classes will only teach counting up to five hundred, writing your name, and obedience to German honesty, industry and politeness." He gave me a Nazi salute, albeit a mocking one.

I giggled.

"It's interesting," he mused half to himself, "how we have always admired everything German. We Poles have tried so very hard to be as German as possible, us Jews in particular ... what a mistake that was."

"So . . ." I frowned. "Does that mean no more study?"

"Don't worry, Hannale. You and Adam must continue your lessons. Some teachers dislike these rules as much as we do. Panna Mislowski is prepared to teach you. But in secret."

"I didn't think Panna was Jewish."

"She's not. She's just a very brave woman."

"Does that mean we'll go to her house?"

He shook his head. "That would be too dangerous. Instead Panna has arranged another house for your lessons. Eva and Alex will also be going."

This was the best news I had heard for weeks.

Adam and Alex were as chummy as me and Eva. Our two families had always been close. Their father, "Uncle" Harry was always fun and "Aunty" Zenia and Mama could have been sisters. What made me happiest was being with Eva. We had sworn that no matter what happened, we would always be best friends.

Eva had given me a note on my birthday. She had written out the beautiful words of friendship from the Book of Ruth in the scriptures: "*Where you go I will go, and where you stay I will stay. Your people will be my people and your God my God.*" We had also given each other good-luck charms that we carried everywhere. I gave Eva a tiny ivory elephant, and she gave me a silver rabbit with pointy ears.

"Is it too much to ask about my gymnastics, Papa? Am I still allowed to enter competitions?"

Papa shook his head. "I don't think so, *bubbala*. But no one can stop you doing it for yourself."

Panna Mislowski's secret school was six blocks away. Adam and I had to walk there. Not only did I have to wear the armband with the blue star, but we also had to carry identity documents.

German soldiers patrolled the streets and they checked everyone's papers. As we were Jewish, they could take us from the streets and send us away. We wouldn't even be allowed to say goodbye to our parents. We would be taken. Just like that.

"If you see any soldiers, try to hide until they go past," were Papa's careful instructions.

Adam and I made our way through the streets. Many of the houses nearby had been bombed, and the roads were strewn with rubble. We climbed over fallen walls and realized how lucky we were that our house had survived the fighting.

Elza followed me and Adam at some distance to make sure we were safe. We had walked four blocks without seeing any soldiers. But as we turned a corner, we saw two heading from the opposite direction.

My heart leapt into my mouth. As they came closer, the taller one stared at my armband. I was sure he was about to stop us.

Adam grabbed my hand. "Come on, Hanna, let's go."

Elza rounded the corner behind us.

"Good morning," she chirped at the soldiers, carefully steering their attention away from me and Adam to herself. We hurried down the road, hoping Elza wouldn't be searched or questioned. But she wasn't Jewish. If they checked her papers, they would probably leave her alone.

Dear Elza. Always such a mensch.

Panna Mislowski had got hold of a small blackboard and chalk and set up a schoolroom using a small table and a few rickety chairs. We wrote on old-fashioned slate boards, as pencils had become too valuable. Food was rationed and hard to find. We always took something for us to eat and also something for Panna. Usually a knob of bread, a scrap of cheese, a few pickled cucumbers. Sometimes a few slices of salted fish. How I longed for Elza's chicken soup with dumplings. Saliva collected in my mouth remembering how good it was.

Eva and I sat at the back of the room, while Alex and Adam were in front.

Those two boys were always dreaming up some new prank. One time they snuck out to the street and banged loudly on the front door with a piece of wood. We got such a fright. We thought the Germans had found us. When we found out it was only Adam and Alex, you should have heard us yell. But I was glad of their silliness. It made the days seem brighter.

Panna Mislowski used to teach Middle School science and mathematics, so she taught us mostly those subjects. She also insisted that we improve our German. She said, "Knowing the language could save your life."

We didn't have much of a chance to learn history or geography, but Panna urged us to read as much as we could for ourselves. She went to great efforts to find us lots of novels. "Books are full of inspiration," she said. "Especially in difficult times." She gave us copies of *The Three Musketeers*, *Robinson Crusoe*, *The Swiss Family Robinson*, *Emil and the Detectives* and *The Scarlet Pimpernel*.

Papa and Zaida stopped going to Kaminsky's Emporium. There was no point. The shop's windows were broken, with glass all over the pavement, horrid signs scrawled on the walls, all our stock was stolen, and, anyway, we were told we no longer owned it.

Jews were ordered to deposit their money in blocked bank accounts. The bank could release no more than two-hundred-and-fifty zlotys per week.

From being rich, we were now dirt poor. We could no longer afford to keep Elza as our housekeeper. She wasn't Jewish, which meant she was no longer allowed to work for us, anyway.

Mama suggested to Elza that she should go back to her family's farm.

Elza looked horrified. "Of course I won't leave you," she said firmly. "You are my family. You have always been so good to me."

"But we can't afford to pay you," Mama said sadly. "The shop is gone, and we have barely any money."

"I don't want money. I won't leave you just because things get hard."

"But if you're caught working for us, you might be sent to prison or even—" Mama tried to explain.

Before she could continue, Elza drew herself up to her full five-foot-six. "No Nazi will tell me what to do." She seemed ready to take on the entire German army.

Both women burst out crying and hugged each other tightly.

The Germans kept issuing orders. We weren't allowed to hear or play anything by the Polish composer, Chopin. We were only allowed to listen to German music and read German authors. All Communist and Jewish writers, actors and musicians were banned.

Until the Germans invaded Poland, I had never thought much about being Jewish. Our family wasn't religious, though we did celebrate the big Jewish holidays. As well as Chanukah and Rosh Hashanah—the Jewish New Year—we marked Passover and Yom Kippur, the Day of Atonement. On those special days, Jewish people were not permitted to work, so Papa closed the Emporium and we spent the days together as a family. Sometimes we celebrated the end of Yom Kippur at an evening meal with the Lublinskis.

Eva's family were more religious than ours. Every Friday night, the eve of Shabbat, they had a special dinner and sometimes I was invited. I really enjoyed the rituals of lighting candles, blessing the sweet egg bread or challah, and tasting the kosher wine. Aunty Zenia always served a traditional meal of chopped liver, fish balls, chicken soup, roast chicken, vegetables and stewed fruit. Eva's family kept a kosher Jewish kitchen, which meant meat and milk dishes were kept separate, they never ate pork or shellfish, and only bought meat from a Jewish butcher.

Now Zaida and Papa spent their days visiting friends. They had a lot more time on their hands since the shop had closed. Papa often came home from these visits with news, good and bad, of what was happening in the war. So far, since Poland had surrendered, it didn't seem much was going on. Only the Germans' continual obsession with us Jews.

More and more people were vanishing. Papa's friend Pan Silverman and his family were among those who had disappeared. We had heard rumours that some people were being sent to labour camps where they were forced to work for the Germans in their war efforts. We heard other rumours that they were being shot.

I tried not to think about it. But then Zaida went out one morning and never came home.

Even though Mama and Papa were always kind and good, no one else was able to comfort me the same way as my grandfather. Now, because he had gone, I needed comforting more than ever. But he wasn't there.

I cried for him every day. The lump in my throat refused

to go away. For a long time I found it too hard to swallow and I barely ate. Mama got worried. She kept saying, "The last thing Zaida will want is for you to get sick."

These days there was never enough food to go around. Papa had the small amount of money he was allowed to take from his savings at the bank. But it was never enough.

He had already traded his gold watch, cufflinks, wedding ring and some of Mama's jewellery for bread, sausage and a few vegetables. We celebrated Adam's eighth birthday with a cake made from one egg, some oil, a little flour and a tiny amount of sugar. Mama's favourite pearl earrings were swapped for those ingredients.

Life in Warsaw was getting harder. Each day I felt Zaida's absence more strongly. He used to wait for me to come home from school to talk about what I'd learnt. Now, every time I came home, his loss hit me again and again.

"Can't we still try to find him?" I begged Papa before I left for Panna Mislowski's school.

His face crumpled as he showed his loss and pain. "We looked everywhere. What else can we do?"

He was right. There was nothing we could do that we hadn't tried already. No one knew anything.

"Be careful on your way to school today, *bubbala*." Papa hugged me and Adam goodbye. "Adam, you must look after your sister."

"We will look after each other, Papa. I promise."

"And I'll look after both," Elza chimed in. "Off we go."

As always, Elza followed from behind, watching us until we safely arrived in Panna's street. Then, before she continued on, she checked that we were inside the house.

"Good morning, Panna," was our usual greeting. I went into the kitchen to leave the food we'd brought. Today, we had a large loaf of bread. It was stale, but there was even enough for Eva and Alex.

We waited in the schoolroom for them to arrive. After an hour, they still hadn't turned up. Panna started to worry. "Continue your reading," she said trying to calm our anxiety. "I'm sure they won't be long."

But Eva and Alex didn't arrive. At lunchtime, I wanted to walk to their house to see where they were.

"No, Hanna," Panna said firmly. "I'd never forgive myself if something happened to you. I can't let you out on your own."

"I'll go," Adam cried.

"No," Panna repeated. "But perhaps it's best if you go home early today."

I took out the note that Eva had given me and reread it. *"Where you go I will go, and where you stay I will stay . . ."*

Oh where, oh where was she?

After the Lublinskis' disappearance, Papa decided we must leave Warsaw. "It's not going to be simple," he said. "No other country is willing to accept us."

"I told you we should have gone to Paris," Mama kept repeating.

"What makes you think the French are any different?"

"They might have accepted us if we'd not left things so late," Mama reminded him.

Papa didn't answer.

The next day he called me and Adam into the dining room. "Elza has suggested we go to the country. To her mother's house."

I gulped. I had always thought Elza's family had been unkind to her. I didn't think her mother would want to help us.

Mama said, "Elza has received a letter from her mother saying she has had an accident. Since Elza's father died, her mother has been running the farm on her own. Now she needs help. Elza thinks that if we offer to help her mother with the chores, maybe she will hide us in return."

"Won't the Germans find us there?" Adam asked.

"How will we get there?" I wanted to know. "Jews aren't allowed to catch trains."

Papa nodded. "You're right. Jews aren't allowed to leave

Warsaw. If the Germans catch us, that will be our death sentence. But if we stay here, who knows what will happen. The Lublinkskis . . . Zaida . . ." His voice, brittle with sorrow, trailed away.

Mama squeezed his hand and turned to us. "Papa and Elza have had an idea." Her smile encouraged Papa to continue.

He roused himself and said, "Elza met her old neighbour Andre in the market yesterday. He has a horse and cart that he uses to carry pigs and sheep into town to sell. If we give him some money, he is prepared to hide us in his cart and take us back to Elza's mother's farm."

"Can we trust him?" I asked.

"We have no other choice."

Father called Elza into the dining room to join us.

She smiled at us reassuringly. "It's all organized," blue eyes crinkling at the corners. "After Andre leaves his pigs at the market, he will come to the alley that runs by the back door. We must be waiting for him, and ready to climb onto his wagon. He will use the animals' straw to hide you. It won't be very comfortable, but I'm sure you can manage."

"Elza will sit beside Andre," Papa added. "If any Germans want to inspect Andre's cart, Elza will try to stop them. There will be manure from the animals in the cart. The smell should put them off."

I screwed up my nose. "We have to lie down on stinky manure?"

"Better a bad smell than stay here, *bubbala*," Mama said. "I know you will be brave."

"How come Andre is prepared to help us?" Adam asked. We all knew that if we were caught, he could also be shot.

"He needs the money," Elza explained. "He wastes all his money gambling and he owes a lot to some thugs. He says they have threatened to kill him if he doesn't pay up."

"But we don't have any more money, do we, Papa?"

"I still have some hidden for a rainy day." He gave a sad smile. "And it seems the Nazis have brought us a thunderstorm."

Leaving Warsaw meant loads of careful planning. We were to leave in two days.

Mama stared around in despair. "What do we take?"

"Only what fits in two small suitcases." Papa's voice brooked no argument.

Mama surveyed her surroundings. Our house was filled with things collected for over sixty years by generations of Kaminskys. There were paintings, sculptures and silverware—cutlery, samovars, tea and coffee sets—beautiful furniture and rugs. We knew that once the word got out that the house was empty, our doors would be smashed in and everything stolen.

Adam was desperate to bring his violin. Papa didn't think it a good idea. He said, "You'll want to play it, and this will attract too much attention."

Adam got so cross he went to his room where he kept playing the same tune over and over until we nearly went mad.

At least I didn't have to pack anything in order to practise gymnastics. I was sure I could find a place to swing from, or something to vault over. I could work on my floor exercises. My pockets also fitted a hankie, my charm bracelet, my gymnastic ribbon, a miniature pack of cards, and, most importantly, my silver rabbit and Eva's note.

I was allowed to pack one warm undershirt, two pairs of underpants, two pairs of socks, one set of warm stockings, one nightgown, and one book into one of the suitcases.

I spent ages deciding which book to take. I had read all of the books Panna Mislowski had given me except Baroness Orczy's *The Scarlet Pimpernel*. I wasn't sure if I should take that, or bring an old favourite. I didn't want to take something too short. Who knew how long we might be hiding on the farm?

I looked at the jacket: "*In 1792, the French Revolution has turned into a Reign of Terror. The streets of Paris are filled with unruly mobs, threatening the aristocracy with death by Madame Guillotine. Their only hope is the dashing Scarlet Pimpernel, a mysterious saviour who whisks the persecuted men, women and children out of danger and across the English Channel to safety. But who could the Scarlet Pimpernel be? A thorn to the French authorities, a rose to all else, no one admires him more than Marguerite Blakeney. The Pimpernel is the exact opposite of her silly husband, the foppish Sir Percy."*

Panna Mislowski had chosen well. I placed the book in the suitcase.

Mama had bought a packet of bleach to dye our hair. One by one she led us to the bathroom to spread bleach over our heads. That bleach was so strong, it stung my eyes and my nostrils. But I stayed as still as I could. Mama washed my hair and called Adam in.

I looked in the mirror. I had thought that my hair might now be the colour of sunlight like the other blonde girls I knew. It wasn't. It was pale orange. I thought it looked strange against my olive skin. I stared at my reflection in dismay.

"Strawberry blonde!" Mama did her best to sound kind. "Just like Ginger Rogers!"

Ginger Rogers was my favourite movie star. She danced like an angel. When I practised my floor routines in gymnastics class, I imagined myself twirling around just as she did with Fred Astaire, elegant and graceful.

"But Ginger Rogers is a real blonde, isn't she, Mama?"

"Nonsense! Why do you think she's called Ginger?"

Andre was due to pick us up at sunrise. We had to get to the other side of Otwock and to Elza's mother's farm before dark. The Germans had placed a curfew on Warsaw and anyone found on the streets or roads at night was shot.

It was still dark when Papa woke us. Mama had already told me what to wear. I put on my warmest dress, though I hated wearing it because the wool prickled, woollen stockings, thick sweater, knitted cap, winter coat and boots. It felt like I was setting off for the Arctic.

Once everyone was ready, we trooped into the kitchen. Mama gave each of us a little bread and cheese, but I couldn't eat. No one could.

We waited for dawn and the sound of a horse and cart.

We heard trams and cars roar and rattle past our house. Voices told us pedestrians were passing by. Some, we knew, had to be soldiers. Footsteps came down the side alley that led into ours. We froze. The footsteps continued past us and faded away.

Ryzia was fussing, desperate to run around. But Papa held her tight.

By now it was daylight.

"Shhhhhhhh!" I said to Ryzia. I was sure I could hear the clip clop of hooves over cobblestones and the rattle of cart wheels. Papa went toward the window and I followed.

The most tired horse I'd ever seen—all skin and ribs, his mane and tail dusty and raggedy as if they'd never been brushed—was pulling a dilapidated cart. It stopped outside our back door.

Elza hurried outside, while we hid in the kitchen in case it was a trap.

She returned, whispering, "Hurry, hurry . . . hardly any time."

We stepped out into the alley. Andre said nothing but nodded at Papa. Papa handed him a package. I supposed that was the money he was promised.

Mama climbed onto the back of the cart first and held out her arms for Ryzia. Papa handed her to Mama as I climbed up. Papa hoisted Adam onto the cart. "Lie down! Quickly!" Elza said in an urgent whisper.

I burrowed under the hay. It stank of animal droppings, but it was dry. Papa climbed up too, and lay down on the other side of Adam, putting his arm protectively around him. Andre spread more hay over us as Elza kept watch. So far, no one had seen us.

I felt the weight of the hay as it was piled over me. It became hard to breathe, and with my finger I made a small tunnel through the hay to let in air. I kept my eyes closed. I couldn't see anything anyway, and the hay and the droppings were making my eyes itch.

The cart began to move. I lay as still as I could, comforting myself by listening to the rhythm of the horse's hooves clopping down the laneway. And then the sound slowed as Andre manoeuvred the cart into the main street. It was a tricky turn, and as the heavy cart banged into the corner of a building, it lurched, and so did I, hitting my head against the hard wood beneath me. I felt a lump begin to form, but I bit my lip and didn't make a sound.

Ryzia began to wail. Adam and I were old enough to know what was going on and what was at stake. She was just a baby. We had no way of making her understand that it was important to be quiet.

She was now crying so loudly, we thought she might wake the entire neighbourhood. Elza jumped off her seat at the front of the cart and took Ryzia from Mama's arms. Luckily, there was no one about to see her or hear us. Elza cradled the baby against a chest as comforting as a bolster; and with Elza's familiar smell, Ryzia settled and then, exhausted, fell asleep.

Very slowly the horse and cart continued along the road that led east. Papa, Mama, Adam and I continued to lie still, not making a sound. We reached the outskirts of the city. The cart came to a stop. I could hear voices, German voices, talking to Andre.

"Where are you going?" a man asked. He didn't sound too interested in knowing the answer. It must be a question he had to ask all passing vehicles.

"Home," answered Andre. "I have just delivered my stock to market."

"That explained the stench then," answered the first voice.

Another man said. "I've seen you before."

"Yes," Andre answered. "I come this way with my livestock every so often."

"Don't recognize the kid though. Yours? Doesn't look a bit like you with that orange hair. You sure you're not a carrot farmer?"

The soldiers were laughing. It was awful hearing them make fun of Ryzia, but at least they didn't sound suspicious.

"She's my niece." It was Elza's voice. "Takes after her father. He's just the same—a real carrot top."

"Poor kid," replied the first soldier. "Well, off you go. Take that stinking cart away from here as fast as you can."

Papa had been right. That smelly manure did indeed help us.

It took the rest of the day to get to Elza's mother's farm. We had to pass through Otwock, go through the town and out again, to get there.

I could hardly believe the relief when the cart finally stopped. My bones ached, my eyes and nose itched, and I was parched. But we had made it.

I climbed out and stretched my cramped limbs. I took in gulps of clean, fresh air.

Only then did I look around. We were at the end of a small drive leading to the farmhouse. Next to it was a barn.

It was still autumn and the sky was filled with light fluffy clouds. Birds darted across the fields to catch insects that quivered above and around them. There were a few late-blooming flowers near the fence that led to the house. Just beyond a clump of tall trees reached for the sky, their leaves already red and gold.

Nothing here hinted of what was happening in Warsaw. Nothing here hinted of war. The countryside was beautiful.

Andre continued up the road.

"Thank you," Papa called after him.

Andre didn't call back.

We walked quietly toward the farmhouse. Elza's mother was not expecting us.

Mama had said that she thought it very unlikely that an anti-Semitic old woman would be prepared to risk her life for Jews. But Elza had replied, "My mama is greedy for money. If Mr. Kaminsky pays her enough, she will hide the devil himself. And she needs help. She is old. And look around you. The farm needs work, a lot of work. She needs money and labour."

Elza was right. As we got closer to the farmhouse, it seemed less picturesque and more like it was about to crumble. The thatched roof of the house was high pitched so snow could slide off easily, but there were gaps in the thatching that needed repair. It looked as if it hadn't been fixed in years. The barn door was swinging off its hinges. Everything needed a fresh coat of paint. The courtyard was thick with mud and the pond covered in slime. Two hens wandered around pecking in the mud searching for something to eat. I didn't think they'd find much.

Just then, the front door of the house opened. An old woman emerged. She held a frying pan over her head like she was ready to club us.

Anya looked exactly like Elza, only the round face under the woollen scarf was more wrinkled. They both had the same blue eyes.

"Mama," Elza said. "It's me. Put down the pan. These are the Kaminskys."

Papa and Elza moved toward Anya. She looked small and old next to Papa. He towered over her.

Anya was frowning. She didn't seem the least bit pleased to see her daughter. Even less pleased to see us.

Mama clutched Ryzia, and Adam and I stood behind her at some distance while Papa, Elza and Anya talked.

Elza said, "Since Papa's death you need my help to run the farm. You can't do it on your own. Pan and Panna Kaminsky offer their help and they will also pay you to stay here. The loft is empty."

The old lady scowled at her daughter. "But what do I do if those Germans come looking around here? We'll all be killed."

"The Kaminskys will stay hidden. And they can help with the farm work."

"How can they do this if they are hiding?" Anya spat at her daughter.

"Farm work can be done before dawn and at dusk. They can come out then to work. The rest of the time they can hide."

Anya grunted.

"And I will help in the fields during the day," Elza quickly added. "No one will suspect anything."

"How did you get here then?"

"Andre brought us in his cart."

"Well, he knows, then. What if he decides to sell your secret? What's in it for him not to?"

"We have to trust him, Mama," Elza said. "We all do. We have no choice."

"Then you have given me no choice," Anya angrily cried.

"The Nazis have given none of us any choice." Papa's voice was soft.

Adam suddenly began to sob, overcome with fear and exhaustion.

Elza must have been able to feel *something,* because on seeing Adam cry, she stopped arguing and told Mama to take us inside.

The house had only one large room, which served as kitchen, living room and bedroom. A large cast-iron stove down the far wall was used to cook on and warm the room.

There was a table, a few chairs and a wooden sofa covered in homespun rugs and shawls. The bed was close to the stove.

The fire in the stove was almost out. As we stood near it hoping to warm ourselves, we watched Elza heap twigs, coal and dried animal droppings inside it. Using bellows, she sent in more air to feed the flames.

Anya had retreated to the bed. She sat there watching us in silence.

Elza took no notice and went off to find water. She came back with two full buckets, two glasses and some very hard mouldy bread and cheese.

As soon as Adam had something to drink and eat, he seemed to recover.

Next, Elza led us up a small flight of rickety steps at the back of the room. She pushed open a door in the roof that led to the loft. The roof was low but pitched. Papa could stand up only in the centre. Mama also had to crouch most of the time. But for me, Adam and Ryzia it wasn't so bad.

"This is where you can live," Elza said. "It's not much, but we'll see what we can do."

There was no furniture, only a bunch of rags in one corner and some straw strewn around the floor.

"We can do something with the things we've brought," Mama's voice was hopeful. "Thank you, Elza."

If the attic was to be our home until the war was over, we knew we had to make the best of it.

Mama took out the clothes we had brought, and we removed all our top layers. Elza and Mama fashioned some bedding out of straw, laying any extra clothes on top as blankets. Mama had brought her beautiful fur coat that her mother had bought for her in Paris. It was long and soft and had ruffles around the neck that kept out the coldest winds. She laid it on top and settled Ryzia into the comforting folds.

"Get some rest," Elza said. "I will go talk to Mother."

We were so tired, we lay down on our makeshift beds. Adam and Ryzia fell asleep straight away. I dozed off listening to my parents whisper to each other. "We will be all right," Papa kept assuring Mama. "We will be all right, Miriam."

A rooster's crow woke me just before dawn.

I lay there, watching slants of light creep into a tiny space between the cottage wall and thatched roof beside my makeshift bed. I got up to look through it into the courtyard and even further toward the fields. I could also see light coming through smaller cracks at the other end of the loft. Crawling as quiet as a spider or an ant, I went to the widest crack and peered outside. From there I glimpsed trees, their leaves rustling and changing colour.

Suddenly there was a tremendous clatter.

My heart leapt into my mouth. Someone was coming upstairs!

*Had the Germans found us already? Had Elza's mother reported us?*

Elza came in carrying two buckets.

"Good morning," she sang. Seeing my startled look, and Papa and Mama rousing themselves, she explained, "We must start early on the farm, as I said. Mother will allow you to stay if you do all the morning and evening chores. You must do them before the sun rises too high."

Papa rubbed his eyes.

Elza set the buckets down, saying to Mama, "One bucket is full of fresh water and the other is your lavatory."

Adam winced. "Do you mean we have to go to the toilet in a bucket?"

"It's the best we can do, for now," she said. "Never get the buckets confused. Does everyone realize how important this is?"

We all nodded. Even Ryzia who was too little to understand.

Elza turned to Papa. "Mr. Kaminsky, I will use some of the money you gave me to buy livestock, a cow, perhaps a few pigs and some poultry. We need to stack the hay and to collect what is left in the field to feed these new animals."

I sat up. "Can me and Adam help?"

Elza looked doubtful. "Hanna, I'm not sure. Not today.

Let's first work out a safe routine. It is very dangerous for you to be seen."

"People might see Papa."

"Perhaps. So we make him look more like us," she suggested. "Mr. Kaminsky, before you come downstairs, please shave your head and your moustache. I will give you my father's old clothes."

Shaved, I hardly recognized him, he looked so strange. Papa's new jacket and pants were threadbare and didn't fit him well. But I think he was happy to be able to help in any way he could. Without Papa having had the foresight to hide cash and Mama's jewellery before the Germans marched into Warsaw, we might not have been here.

The next few mornings and evenings Papa helped Elza store what was left of the hay. He left the loft before sunrise and came back just after first light. At sunset he left again, returning later in the evening exhausted, his face and hands covered in grime, his fingernails rimmed with dirt.

Other than Papa doing the chores, Elza had warned the rest of us not to go downstairs, not yet. We didn't see or speak to Anya. Part of the bargain Elza and Papa had made with Anya was that we never bother her and that we remain hidden.

After three days Elza allowed me and Adam to go downstairs.

"If you are very quiet, you may sit by the stove."

Anya was already there. She didn't look up. Her dog, Spotty, sat by her side. He had a black coat spotted with white freckles. He was old and half blind, but he seemed friendly enough. I put out my hand so he could sniff it. He licked my fingers, and I scratched behind his ears.

Anya grunted at Spotty, so I sat down by the stove. I had brought my cards, and I began to play Patience. Adam watched for a while, and then we played together without speaking, balancing the cards against each other to build a house. It was the quietest thing we could think to do.

The next morning Elza went to the market to get the animals she had mentioned. Papa's money would be used to buy a cow, two pigs, four hens and three ducks. They were to live and sleep in the barn next to the house. Watching out for her return, I peered through the gap down to the courtyard.

As soon as I glimpsed the animals, I couldn't suppress a shriek of joy. Adam was nervous about having to be so near a cow, but I knew how placid they were.

"I hope I don't have to milk it," he whispered.

"I hope I do!" I cried.

Even Mama, who doesn't usually like being in close contact with animals, smiled. "Perhaps that could be your morning chore, Hanna."

I watched Elza take the animals into the barn. She came to the loft a few minutes later. "Mr. Kaminsky, I wanted to buy a horse, but the Germans have taken every single one."

Papa blinked. "Why do we need a horse?"

"Next spring," she explained. "A horse will help with the ploughing."

Mama's smile disappeared. "Do you think we will still be here next spring?"

No one answered. The future was a question mark. Who knew what it held, and if there might come a time when we no longer had to hide.

Adam and I were allowed outside the house in the half-hour before sunrise and again just after dusk. The poultry roamed the yard during the day but were locked in at night.

"Hanna," Elza said. "It'll be your job to feed those six hens and the three ducks. You have to collect their eggs, and make sure the fox can't find them. Adam, you're to help round them up for the night."

At first, we had no idea how to collect those birds. Any time we tried to get close they tried to peck us. After one time too many of being chased by a rooster rather than the other way around, I said, "Adam, we're bigger and stronger than those birds, aren't we?"

He nodded.

I took a deep breath. "So they'd better know who is boss."

He giggled.

After that, any time a hen or the rooster, a duck or a drake, tried to peck me, I gave them a tiny smack. Not enough to hurt, but enough to make them stop.

Very soon all I had to do was raise a hand and they knew to behave.

We named some of the hens. My favourite I called Marguerite after the beautiful heroine, a French actress, in *The Scarlet Pimpernel*. I had already finished it. I was so glad that I had picked that book to bring to the farm. It was wonderful.

Marguerite was the best egg-layer and she always let me pick her up and stroke her lovely brown feathers. The noisy bossy rooster I named Chauvelin, after the villain in the book. The ducks spent most of their time in the muddy pool at the end of the yard that was rapidly icing over. Because the drake was bad tempered and harassed the ducks, Adam wanted to call him Adolf, after the German Führer, Adolf Hitler.

I was horrified. "No! Not even the most horrid duck deserves that."

We agreed to call him Sheriff, after the Sheriff of Nottingham in *The Adventures of Robin Hood*. That was Adam's favourite movie.

The sow Elza bought was soon to have babies. She was huge. I was looking forward to playing with those piglets when they finally appeared.

"Don't get too attached," Elza warned me. "There are reports that the Germans are taking animals from some farms close by."

"But what if they do? What if they find us?" I asked, scared.

Elza patted my shoulder to comfort me. "If they do come, they'll be happy to take our animals and leave us alone."

She taught me how to milk the cow. We had named her Daisy. As I pulled Daisy's udders and milk came spurting out, I rested my head against her flank. This felt so warm and comforting, she must have known how much I liked her. She was sweet and gentle and never tried to kick me or the milk bucket.

Once the morning chores were done, we were under strict instruction to return upstairs, to stay hidden, and to be as quiet as possible.

Papa had packed two slates, a few pieces of chalk and a textbook in one of our suitcases. He was determined to teach us mathematics and science. Straight after morning chores, Papa led us through our lessons. Then he played with Ryzia, and Mama talked to us about music, humming her favourite pieces. Adam pretended to play them on a violin, arms held out as if holding an instrument, his right hand moving smoothly up and down as if running a bow across the strings.

In the afternoon I filled the long hours playing cards and reading. I had read *The Scarlet Pimpernel* three times already.

I wasn't bored rereading it. The story engrossed me and I boasted to Papa, "I know some of it off by heart." To prove this, I quoted, "*Thus human beings judge of one another, superficially, casually, throwing contempt on one another, with but little reason, and no charity.*"

"Yes, yes," Papa said. "Think about how many ideas you have learnt. Can you tell them to me?"

I thought hard. "I now know that history repeats."

"Yes, *bubbala*? In what way?"

"Well, just as the Nazis blame all Jews for the problems in Germany, and the poverty there after the war, the French blamed all the nobility for their poverty and rounded them up to be killed."

His nod was approving. "Interesting, Hanna. Go on."

"The French wanted to kill or imprison everyone of noble birth. They didn't discriminate. They just blamed them all. So the aristocracy had to try to escape."

"Just like us?" Adam asked.

"Yes," I said. "Although a lot of them didn't get away. They were sent to the guillotine."

"But some did get away," Adam insisted.

"Yes! And in the book, it is the Scarlet Pimpernel who saves them."

"And how does he do that, Hanna?" Papa asked.

"He has a band of friends who help him, and they undertake daring rescues together. He even smuggles people, by hiding them in old carts, just the way we escaped Warsaw! Only his friends know his identity. He is, in fact, Sir Percy Blakeney, an English aristocrat. Everyone believes he is a fool only interested in clothes and gambling."

Adam was captivated by this story. "Is he a fool?"

"No, that's just a disguise. He's quite, quite brilliant!"

"Does he rescue people from the guillotine?"

"He does! And each time he leaves a card, with a picture of a flower on it—a scarlet pimpernel."

"Don't the French catch him?"

"They try, but he's far too clever. He is a skilled sword-fighter and can take on wonderful disguises. He always manages to escape the trickiest of situations."

"Can I read that book too?" Adam asked.

"Of course," nodded Papa. "I think that's a marvellous idea, don't you, Hanna?"

I longed to practise my gymnastics. In my imagination, I sprinted down a runway, vaulted from a springboard over a wooden horse and arms raised, landed on both feet. On an imaginary beam, I ran, skipped, did forward and backward circles. Hanging from a bar with both hands, then only one, I swung into different positions . . .

If only!

But in a loft there is only room to move around very quietly. Besides, even when I accidently made a tiny, tiny noise, Anya would hit the ceiling with her stick.

At least I could use my gymnastics ribbon without making a sound. If I sat on my patch of bedding, I could fling the ribbon upwards, twirling it under the highest part of the roof, making it dance. The ribbon unfurled, curled and undulated. It fascinated Ryzia and was a wonderful way of calming her when she became fretful.

We established a routine that made our life tolerable, and comfortingly predictable. At dusk, Papa, Adam and I headed downstairs and out of the house—me and Adam to round up the animals for the evening, Papa to do whatever needed doing in the evening light.

At night, we had a few oil lamps and candles if we needed them, but these had to be carefully conserved. We ate by the light of one candle, and then settled in our makeshift nests of clothes to sleep.

Being on the farm meant we had enough to eat. Anya and Elza cooked a porridge called kasha made from buckwheat. Mama and I also helped pickle cabbage, beets, turnips, corn and cucumbers and store potatoes. We sliced cabbages, and placed cucumbers in clay jars and poured salty water over them. We made jam out of sour cherries and berries.

Adam and I looked for pine mushrooms underneath

the trees behind the house that might have survived under the first layer of snow. This brown yellow fungus had to be picked very quickly or it turned a weird greenish-blue. Elza warned us to keep away from anything red and spotty as those toadstools were poisonous.

Sometimes when we were mushroom gathering I found a clear space between pines where the thin snow wasn't too soft or too hard. While Adam kept watch, I took off my coat and boots and practised forward and backward cartwheels.

Pickled vegetables, mushrooms, a few boiled potatoes, and sometimes a slice of rye bread topped with sour cherry jam, kept hunger at bay. Most of the milk and eggs went with Elza to sell at the market, but occasionally we kept some. We had no meat. Any meat Elza could afford, she reserved for Anya.

"Keeps the old lady happy," she said with her abrupt laugh, "even though she's hardly got a tooth to chew with."

We didn't miss meat all that much—those pine mushrooms, sliced and fried, tasted almost the same. Sometimes Adam complained. Mama said he was hungry for meat because he was growing so quickly. When she measured him against me, he was nearly my height though he was three years younger. We decided that he was most likely going to end up as tall as Papa.

# 1940

Adam and I were getting used to life on the farm. Our bodies were still strong as we had food and could exercise, but our clothes were dirty and torn.

Winter had set in and snow covered the fields. There was less for Papa to do, though our animals still needed to be fed, to be let out, and their stalls cleaned.

Elza became worried about footprints. The soft snow showed where we had been and how many people tramped around the farm.

"Follow me," she said, leading the way to the barn. "Step in my footsteps." Elza's boots left large dents in the snow. Adam and I made sure that we stepped inside her prints, and didn't leave any extra marks.

The loft was so bitterly cold that Anya allowed us to sit by the stove at night. Not for long. Just long enough to warm ourselves before going to sleep. Our bedding had lessened as we now wore most of our clothes rather than using them as blankets. We slept in one clump, Mama and Papa on the outside, Ryzia curled inside Mama's fur coat, me and Adam beside her, this way sharing what little body warmth we had. My nose felt like an icicle and I had to rub and rub to give it some feeling.

In the mornings I crept to the crack between the loft floor and the thatching to look out at the trees behind the house. Those trees dressed in their overnight coat of glistening snow reflected the bright morning sunshine. It was like those stories I read about when I was little, far away lands where you could find gnomes, fairies and elves if you looked long and hard enough.

Even though there was no chance of finding mushrooms, sometimes at dusk for some air and exercise and to get us out of the loft, Elza allowed me and Adam to follow in her footsteps to where trees seemed to stretch right into the sky. Under the pale grey winter light, if you looked straight up, it was hard to tell where their snowy branches ended and the sky began.

One afternoon I couldn't find my silver rabbit, the one Eva had given me, anywhere. I had obviously dropped it somewhere in the snow. I was so upset I cried for hours.

Sometimes I woke in the middle of the night thinking of Zaida. I thought I heard him calling "Hannale . . . Hannale." Then I opened my eyes half expecting to see his pince-nez, his little goatee beard, his immaculately turned-out person, and smell his distinctive odour of cologne and cigars.

But once fully awake, the slow realization came that I would never see him again and tears ran down my cheeks. What had happened to him? What had happened to the Lublinskis? What would happen to us?

Then I slept and dreamt again.

Anya had taken an unexpected liking to Adam. She started asking Elza to send him downstairs to talk to her.

When I questioned Elza about this, she said, "He reminds her of my brother Marck."

Elza's brother Marek had been conscripted into the Polish Army when the call for able-bodied men had gone out. It wasn't certain, though highly probable, that he'd been taken prisoner when Poland surrendered to both the Nazis and the Russians. Either that, or he was dead. No one had heard anything from him since he had left the farm in September 1939. Though Elza wasn't particularly fond of either her mother or of Marek, her kind heart couldn't help feeling some anguish.

While Anya paid attention to Adam, she could not tolerate Ryzia. Even Mama coming downstairs to collect water or hang Ryzia's diaper rags around the stove made her scowl and mutter curses. Poor Mama and Ryzia had no choice but to avoid the old lady completely. Unlike Papa, Adam and I, they were confined to the loft almost completely. I can't imagine how they coped. The roof was so short except in the middle, Mama had to stoop to get around. What kept me sane was getting out with the animals and amongst the trees, breathing crisp fresh air.

I know Papa was worried about Mama. She was getting more and more unhappy. Ryzia was almost too young to know anything different, and Adam, Anya's favourite, seemed to live only in his own world. He continued to play his pretend violin and hum the music only he heard in his head.

I lost myself reading and rereading *The Scarlet Pimpernel*. I knew it almost by heart, as if the words had entered me and we were one. I twirled my ribbon in the rafters of the loft, and pretended I was Lady Marguerite at a fancy ball, dressed in a fine Parisian gown, my hair piled up on top of my head in auburn curls.

But of course my hair was nothing of the sort. Since we left Warsaw and our hair was starting to grow out, we had looked very strange. We were more likely to draw attention to ourselves with brown hair sprouting from our scalps and a definite line to where it changed to pale orange. Soon after we arrived on the farm, Mama began chopping off the ends and more orange came off every week. Now everyone's hair was brown, but mine was still short. Thank goodness the cutting had stopped and I could look normal again. Not that anyone cared or saw me. The whole point was not to be seen.

Most days I spent on my makeshift bed curled up with my book.

I read: "*Recently a very great number of aristos had succeeded in escaping out of France and in reaching England safely. There were curious rumours about these escapes; they had become very frequent and singularly daring; the people's minds were becoming strangely excited about it all. It was asserted that these escapes were organized by a band of Englishmen, whose daring seemed to be unparalleled, and who, from sheer desire to meddle in what did not concern them, spent their spare time in snatching away lawful victims destined for Madame la Guillotine. These rumours soon grew in extravagance; there was no doubt that this band of meddlesome Englishmen did exist; moreover, they seemed to be under the leadership of a man whose pluck and audacity were almost fabulous. Strange stories were afloat of how he and those aristos whom he rescued became suddenly invisible as they reached the barricades and escaped out of the gates by sheer super-natural agency . . .*"

"*Pluck and audacity.*" If only I had those qualities. How I wished I could do something more than hide in this loft and feel sorry for myself.

Winter seemed endless. Every morning after I woke, I crawled to the gap between wall and thatching to look outside. At last one day I saw signs of spring: the sun rising earlier; patches of brown where the snow was starting to melt; our animals becoming restless.

As the weeks wore on, and the weather grew warmer, Elza resumed her trips to the market in Otwock. As she was our only contact with the outside world, I asked her to describe that town for me.

Elza put down the clean buckets she had brought up to the loft. "There are some splendid buildings. There's a lovely old theatre, the City Hall and the City Museum."

"What else?" I was as eager for information as I was to be back in my old life in Warsaw.

She smiled, the skin crinkling around her eyes. "Churches, markets, lots of houses, cottages, a train station. The usual."

"Are there shops?"

She seemed surprised I even asked. "Of course! Lots. Bakeries, butchers, greengrocers, stores where you can buy clothes, shoes and linen. But really for anything else you have to travel to Warsaw." She paused. "Most of those shops were Jewish. They're closed now."

"Do any Jews still live there?"

"Yes. Many, maybe about twelve thousand."

"Are they safe?" Mama sounded hopeful. "They must be if they did not leave? Romek, is there a reason we can't live safely in Otwock? Perhaps the danger has passed?"

Instead of answering, Papa's brow wrinkled and he turned away.

Elza shook her head. "Since the German invasion, they've been pushed into one small district of the town."

"A ghetto?" Mama asked.

"Yes." Elza's face fell.

"What else is happening to them?" Mama's face was anxious. "Could you find out?"

"I can try," Elza replied. "But I don't think it's a good idea to ask too many questions."

A week later, she returned from the market with some more information. "I heard reports that Jewish people, whole families, were being placed on trains and sent away."

"Where to?" asked Papa.

Elza paused before saying, "There's talk of camps."

"What sort of camps?"

She shrugged. "Labour camps I guess. Where you work for food and shelter. I guess they are made to help in the war effort."

"Slavery," Papa muttered.

Mama shuddered. Just the thought of it was like bringing winter back, and we felt chilled to the bone.

The weather was becoming warmer, and we could now go out in the forest at dusk without fear of leaving footsteps. I ached to practise cartwheels and stretch my limbs. I found a patch between the trees and ran through them before placing my hands on the ground and wheeling: one, two, three . . .

I stopped. Something glinted in the fading light beneath one of the silver birch trees. My heart leapt. It was my precious rabbit, the one Eva had given me I thought I had lost forever. I felt happier than I could remember. Surely this was a sign? Maybe this meant Eva was still alive?

Next morning, as Adam and I scrambled to get ready to creep down to the barn for the morning chores, we heard voices downstairs.

One was definitely a man's. I knew it couldn't be Papa because he was still in the loft.

I looked through the gap and saw a horse and a big black dog, a German shepherd, with slobbery jaws. I knew these dogs were used by police to chase criminals.

Spotty didn't like that dog. She started to bark and didn't stop.

We froze.

Thankfully, Ryzia was still asleep.

From downstairs I heard, "Good to see you home, Elza. Your mother needs all the help you can give her."

"Happy to see you too, Jarek." But from Elza's dry tone I knew she really wasn't.

The man said, "Saw a couple of kids near the back of your farm. Out in the trees one morning. A young girl, I think. She was running about. There was another kid with her. Have you seen them?"

Elza paused before saying, "Oh, that must've been Henrik. My cousin from Lodz. We put up him and his kids while he had some business in Otwock. In return he was helping me stack hay."

"Didn't know you had a cousin in Lodz." The man gave a hoarse laugh. "You wouldn't want to be hidin' anyone, would you?"

"Don't know what you're talking about," Elza said tersely.

"Didn't you work for Jews in Warsaw?"

"Don't know what you're on about. Anyway, I'm here now, aren't I?"

Spotty kept barking. I knew she was warning that German shepherd to stay clear. There can't have been any love lost between Elza and Jarek either, because her tone stayed distant though polite. "To what do we owe this visit?"

"Well, now you're talking." He sounded pleased. "I came about that land you're still refusing to sell me . . ."

There was a long pause before, "Which piece exactly are you after?"

The door closed behind them.

Their voices drifted away.

In the long silence that followed, my heart thumped in my ears.

Only when we dared breathe again did I peer through the gap between the wall and thatch. Elza and Jarek were walking toward the horse tethered to the fence, that German shepherd loping behind them.

By the time summer arrived, Ryzia had turned into a charming toddler, though she was small. We all were I guess, as there was enough to eat to stay alive, but never enough to grow strong. Ryzia was such a chatterbox it was sometimes hard living in the same room and trying to stay calm. But she adored us and showed this by climbing onto our knees and covering us with kisses and hugs. When she got frustrated by not being able to run around, I tried to keep her amused by playing Hide and Seek and Hide the Thimble, not that we had any thimbles to hide, but we made do with my lucky silver rabbit.

Thankfully, Anya was changing too. Where once she couldn't bear the sound of a baby, she now took the same liking to Ryzia as she had to Adam. It was hard not to. Ryzia was a little ball of sunshine. I marvelled at the way she had adapted to living the way we did, even if she could hardly remember anything different.

Anya allowed Adam to bring her downstairs and let her run about.

She skipped to and fro, stopping to drop kisses on Anya's wrinkled cheek. Even Mama agreed that Anya was softening, and that we had Ryzia to thank for it.

Anya never softened to me. But she no longer scowled at me, either.

The animals were growing too. The six piglets were now bigger, and no longer babies. They grunted at Adam and me when we approached, but their grunts were friendly as they knew us well.

Spotty, the chickens and ducks, Daisy and the pigs, they almost felt like family now. Elza warned me that it was never a good idea to get too fond of animals on a farm. But how could I not? There was no one else to talk to.

Papa insisted that we stick to our routine. So every day after we completed our chores, we continued to work on our math and science. He said, "Even though we don't have more books, I am able to tell you about the ones I have read. You can tell me about those you have read. And Mama and Adam and Elza can do the same. When we run out of stories, we will make up our own. Imagination is a powerful tool, never forget that."

Summer turned into autumn. One day led into the next without much change, but I could watch the seasons through the gap between wall and thatch. Leaves turned red and yellow, finally scattering onto the ground to form crisp brown rugs.

As the days got colder, frost sat on the grass when I crept from the house to the barn to feed the animals. And then the cold truly set in and snow covered everything. We prepared ourselves for a second winter huddling together as we hid in the loft.

Elza returned from Otwock one night and asked us to come and join her and Anya by the fire.

"I'm worried," she said. "The news isn't good."

Papa paused a moment before asking, "What have you heard?"

"The Nazis have forced all the Jews in Warsaw to an area in the north. They've created a ghetto."

Mama gasped.

"Go on," Papa urged.

"They are calling it the Jewish Residential Area. But it's not. It's a prison. There's a wall around it, nine feet high with barbed wire on top. Anyone who tries to escape is shot." Tears dripped down Elza's cheeks as she told us.

"But how can that be!" Mama exclaimed. "If all the Jews are there, how can they live in such a space? How big is it?"

Papa remained very quiet.

"It's not very big," Elza said. "It couldn't be more than a couple of square miles." Her head shook with despair. "I don't know!"

Papa finally spoke. "I doubt many of us got out of the city. We were lucky. If most of the Jewish population are there, it must be nearly four hundred thousand people."

"But that's dreadful, Romek," Mama cried. "What will happen to them?"

"I doubt they can survive. With that level of overcrowding, disease will be rampant, and food scarce."

"There are rations in force." Elza kept her voice low in a vain attempt not to frighten us anymore. "Jews are to eat less than two hundred calories a day."

"But then they will starve," Mama cried.

We just looked at each other.

We were so grateful to Elza. And also to Anya. Hiding in the loft was dreadful, but we had enough food and shelter, and best of all, we had each other. I couldn't begin to imagine what life must be like in the ghetto. It must be unbearable.

The nights were growing colder. I thought I might be able to warm myself practising gymnastics. Perhaps exercising would help my toes and fingers to unfreeze? After barely sleeping on the icy-cold floor, I woke early and carefully lifted myself out of the pile of huddled bodies.

Adam whispered, "Where are you going?"

"To the barn! I'm freezing. I want to run around a bit."

"I'll come too," he whispered back.

We tiptoed downstairs, leaving Papa, Mama and Ryzia asleep. We could hear Anya snoring in her bed near the unlit stove. Elza was nowhere to be seen.

We found her in the barn milking Daisy.

"I thought that was my job," I teased her.

She smiled, resting her head on Daisy's side. "I thought we could use some warm milk. Do you want to try some gymnastics?"

"Yes, anything to get warmer."

"I'll chase you!" Adam cried, and I took off to the back of the barn, him close behind me as Marguerite, Chauvelin and Sheriff and the other birds set up a tremendous din.

Adam and I raced up and down the length of the barn, laughing and almost forgetting where we were and why we were there. I felt much warmer on the outside and on the inside, too. I hadn't felt this carefree in ages.

Suddenly, Spotty was barking from the house. Elza looked up. Spotty rarely barked. Anya would never put up with it.

This was a warning!

"Hide! Wherever you can," Elza hissed.

Adam and I lost no time running to the end of the barn

and covering ourselves with hay. My breath came out in short sharp pants.

Once Elza knew we were out of sight, she peered out of the barn door. "Germans," she whispered. "Two German trucks."

We could hear them come to a halt just outside the barn. From inside the house, Spotty was barking madly. I was sure all that noise would wake Papa and Mama. But if the Germans went inside, surely they'd be found? I couldn't bear to think about it.

The animals sensed something was wrong. The pigs grunted and snorted and pushed at their stall wall; the fowls flapped their wings and screeched.

The barn door sprang open with a loud squeal.

Elza strode to the door to demand, "What do you want?"

The soldier wasted no time with introductions, "We have orders to take your livestock," a deep, clipped, voice said. "Werner, Schmitt, take the cow and the pigs. You two, round up the birds."

Elza began to object. "You can't take—"

She was cut off, quickly. "Shut up! Get out of the way!" The voice was menacing. Aggressive.

Elza was quiet after that. I didn't know if she had meekly submitted, or if they had hit her. It wasn't like her to give up without a fight.

By now, Chauvelin was making such a racket, it was hard to hear anything.

There was a lot of movement, animals being captured and under their loud protests, they were led outside.

All this time Adam and I stayed as still as possible. We tried not to breathe. I heard those trucks' engines start up, and then drive down the road away from the farm. We could still hear Chauvelin's indignant squawking, but soon the sound grew faint.

We waited a minute or two more before it felt safe enough to emerge.

We found Elza on the floor of the barn. Her eyes were closed and she didn't move.

"Is she dead?" Adam voiced my own fears.

We ran over to her. She was breathing, but unconscious. She had the beginnings of a large bruise on her temple. Thankfully, no blood.

Papa appeared through the barn door. "Adam! Hanna! Are you all right?"

We nodded.

He knelt beside Elza, placed his fingers on her neck and took her pulse. "She's still alive but unconscious. Help me get her into the house. We must make her warmer."

"Yes, Papa." Adam and I took hold of Elza's legs, while Papa lifted her from under her arms. We carried her like that to the house. Anya and Mama had restarted the stove and moved the bed beside it.

Once again, Elza had saved us.

# 1941

In the next few months, everything changed. Without our animals, we no longer had the milk and eggs they provided, either to eat or trade. Adam and I didn't have any morning chores. I missed the sense of purpose the animals had given me. Oh, and how I missed gentle Daisy. Those kind, docile eyes that used to greet me in the mornings. And Sherriff, the bossy drake . . . those innocent animals had been such a comfort. Without them, it was hard not to feel miserable.

We needed to be far more careful about conserving food. Elza tried to barter jars of cucumbers and cabbage for bread. But everyone else had enough pickled vegetables, and no one was interested in buying more.

Potatoes we did have, but some turned out to be rotten. Sometimes we boiled them and turned them into pancakes. If we were lucky, they didn't make us sick. Sometimes they did.

I spent a lot of time looking through the cracks in our loft. All I saw was snow coming down fast, piling up against the walls. Whirling down from the ash sky, those flakes cast big fat moth-like shadows fluttering aimlessly about, doing their best to smother us in a giant grey cushion.

At night on my thin layer of straw, it was too cold to sleep. I stared into the dark and tried to pretend I was back home on my comfortable mattress in my bed with its blue headboard, looking across the room at shelves filled with toys and books, and walking on thick rugs that sat on pale wooden boards. From there I roamed into the front rooms where the iron stove kept us wonderfully warm. I stared up at our ceiling to admire the ornate lamps, delicately painted cornices and central roses. After listening to Mama on the piano playing Tchaikovsky and Chopin, I headed into a kitchen always filled with the most delicious smells of frying schnitzel, chicken stew, beef goulash, apple strudel and my very favourite cinnamon and chocolate babka.

Then I pictured myself back in my gymnastic class, my teacher showing me how to tackle forward and backward tumbles on the beam. I needed to know how to perfect my straddle jumps, twist moves and circles. If the hardest thing was landing on the ground without stumbling, in my mind I always got that right.

Papa kept reminding me that my imagination was a powerful tool, so I tried to use it as best I could to fight off my growing misery. Though it didn't always work, very occasionally it did.

I continued to read and reread my book. It was the only thing I could do to soak up the hours. Then I was just like Sir Percy in *The Scarlet Pimpernel*. "*Pluck and audacity,*" I repeated picturing myself offering snuff to a German officer. While he sneezes and sneezes, I spirit our family to safety right under his nose. I could save Elza and poor Daisy and the animals. I could be just like Sir Percy, but without having to wear a mask. Where Sir Percy disguised his heroism with vanity and folly, I could also disguise myself. Who would ever suspect me, a twelve-year old girl, as capable of saving anyone from the Nazis?

Late one evening, another visitor arrived. It was Andre. He had turned up to confront Elza. "Are they still here?" he demanded.

"What do you mean?"

"You know exactly what I mean." His voice was harsh. "The Jews. Are they still here?"

His words travelled up to the loft. Each one of them struck fear into us.

"And if they are," Elza replied "what is to you?"

"I've got nothing. Nothing left. Nothing but debts that is." Andre's tone grew quieter.

"None of us have anything." Even kind Elza had grown bitter. "The Germans have made sure of that."

"Your Jews . . . They were rich. I saw where they lived. I know they have money."

"It was taken away from them too, Andre. They were desperate."

"I'm desperate now too. I've no cows to milk, no stock to take to market." His voice suddenly grew ominous. "The only thing I've got to sell is your secret."

"You know what that would mean, Andre," Anya broke in. "You couldn't! We'd all be shot! You are prepared to do that to us, your neighbours? You've known us all your life. You would do that to settle a few debts?"

"No, no, no." There was a pause. "I don't know. I don't know what to do."

All this time Papa had stood like a statue at the door of the loft. His face was still, unreadable. I looked at Mama. She clutched Ryzia and Adam to her side, and her eyes filled with tears.

Papa suddenly opened the door. Before anyone could stop him, he went downstairs. "I can give you whatever I have left," he announced. "Take it. Take all of it. But it buys your silence. If not for us, then for Elza and Anya's sake. Agreed?"

Andre didn't answer.

"Andre?" Elza pleaded.

"Yes. Agreed." And with that we heard the front door close. Papa beckoned us to come downstairs.

"Can we trust him?" Mama asked.

"I don't know. What do you think, Elza?"

Elza looked nervous. "He brought you here, and took a great risk to do so. And he's kept the secret for a long time, nearly two years."

Anya spoke. "He wants money. That's why he did it. That's why he took the risk. And after this money runs out, why still take the risk?"

"She is right," Papa said. "And it seems there may be a reward for turning us in."

"He's a gambler," Elza said. "Always has been. He has a good heart, but the gambling has knocked any sense out of him."

"It's not just him we have to worry about," Anya said. "Jarek has his eye on us too. I'm not selling my farm to him and he knows it."

"He showed up again, last week, prowling around the fields," Elza said. She looked at Papa. "I hadn't wanted to worry you."

"He's a crook," Anya hissed.

"I told him again that Mama will never sell," Elza told us. "And what he could do with his money. What use to us is money when there's no food to buy—or nowhere to live?"

"He is an angry man," Papa mused. "Angry men are dangerous."

Mama was crying. "Romek, what should we do? Where are we to go?"

"Could we hide in the forest?" Adam suggested.

"Not in winter. We'll freeze to death. Perhaps, if it were summer, we could stand a chance."

"What do we do, Papa? I asked, repeating Mama's question. Tears rolled down my face. "Is there anything we can do?"

"We can only wait and see," Papa answered. "Wait and see."

I took Papa's words quite literally and spent the next day waiting and watching the world outside through that crack. There wasn't much to see. Most of the birds had already flown south. Everything I looked at seemed to have turned either black, grey or white in the pale winter light. Charcoal clouds hung heavily. The pine trees were covered in snow. They remained like a last remnant of beauty.

I tried to remember the fields as a riot of poppies, carnations, sunflowers, daisies and violets that blossomed when autumn and winter were over and a fresh spring breeze filled the air. That helped remove some of my fear.

I resumed my watch next morning. Mama tried to coax me away from the crack, but I insisted. Once again, grey clouds blocked out any sunlight and the courtyard was lifeless and still.

In the late morning, the stillness was interrupted by the arrival of a truck. The truck bore the Nazi insignias and flag.

I let out a warning cry.

We had been betrayed.

Our first night in the ghetto in Zelazna Street, our room was cold and noisy; however, it was the first in a long time we hadn't gone to bed starving. The food we bought at the markets meant we ate more that evening than in months.

Papa was determined to improve our living conditions. Next day he went out at dawn and didn't return until five hours later, pulling a small cart filled with furniture.

He had bought a small table, four wooden chairs, five straw mattresses, an old tin bath and best of all, a small stove for cooking and warming water so we could wash both ourselves and our clothes.

Mama stared at these articles in disbelief before asking, "Romek, how on earth did you manage it?"

"Not everyone in the ghetto is poor," he told her placing the table in the centre of the room. "Some make pots of money. They bring food and goods into the ghetto. Some smugglers are so rich, they live like kings." He settled four chairs around the table before continuing, "Even though many people beg for food, these smugglers live in luxurious apartments on Chlodna Street." He looked around for a moment before adding, "You can see them in the Café Hirschfield. I'm told you can buy almost anything there. Gold, diamonds, any food you fancy, ration cards, even forged identity papers."

Mama ran her hand over the table as if to assure herself it really did exist. "Don't the Germans know? How do the smugglers get away with it?"

"Bribery." Papa smiled grimly. "They've made more than enough money to bribe just about anyone."

He had also bought several buckets, one to bring in water, the other as a chamber pot so we didn't always have to use the lavatory at the end of our floor. Each floor in the building had a tap giving fresh water and a lavatory, though the lavatory's smell was so bad I hardly ever went there. Our floor consisted of five lots of rooms housing at least twenty to thirty people. One tap and one lavatory for so many people led to lots of arguments.

The table Papa brought home had uneven legs, so eventually he propped it up with an old copy of the *Gazeta Zydowska*. This was the Jewish newspaper published with the approval of the Germans. I read bits of it when we weren't using the table. It was full of questions about forbidden activities, and these included almost everything. The middle pages had short stories and poetry, mostly about what it was like to live in the ghetto. Thankfully, writing poetry wasn't forbidden. At least, not yet!

After I spent two days helping Mama set up our rooms, I was desperate to walk outside. I needed fresh air. One improvement from living on the farm was being able to go outside without worrying I'd be seen. I persuaded Mama and Papa that I wouldn't speak to strangers and I'd keep a sharp watch for any Germans walking or driving past.

Though Mama insisted this mightn't be safe, Papa said,

"All right, Hanna. But only for a while. Tomorrow, you can take Adam with you, as I will be starting work at the Council." He turned to Adam. "Today you can come with me to the market."

I walked down Zelazna Street, and turned right. So far all I had seen of the ghetto was colourless—just shades of grey, charcoal and black. People's clothes were so shabby; any colour seemed totally drained away. I was missing anything green, anything to do with nature.

The air itself felt grey too, sooty from the coal used for cooking and heating. Even so, being outside on my own and with food in my stomach, I felt a sudden rush of freedom. My body was ready to run, hop and jump. Only I still didn't know if I could.

I tried running a few steps. Then picked up speed. Yes, I could still run. I ran to the end of the street, turned back and ran some more.

Even if I had to dodge people coming in the opposite direction, and the homeless sheltering inside doorways, it felt wonderful. If there was enough space, I felt sure I could manage a cartwheel. I ran a small distance, raised my hands ready to place them on the ground, and then bumped into a man coming the other way. Instead of landing on my hands, I fell onto my knees. I was already out of breath. I needed to regain some stamina.

"Hey, Hanna!" someone called.

It was Karol: one of the boys I'd met when we arrived. Jacob and Moshe, his friends, were with him.

"What are you tryin' to do?"

"A cartwheel." My eyes narrowed. "What's it to you?"

"Is that something you can do?

"Yes. I used to be a gymnast." I bit my lip. "But I'm rusty. I need to practise, and for that I need space, lots more space."

Karol turned his back on me and all three went into a huddle. I didn't know whether to stay or run. In the end I was too curious to leave. What were they talking about?

After a minute, Jacob turned back, a wide grin splitting his face. He said, "We was thinking . . . there's lots of cafés and halls in the ghetto. There's even a theatre close by called the Weisman. Is that the sorta space you want?"

My eyebrows shot up in disbelief.

"We'll see if we can find you something," he went on. And with that, all three took off down the street.

"Well, thanks . . ." I called as they disappeared into the crowd.

I still didn't see how they could help me find enough room to practise. The ghetto overflowed with people. Every available space seemed to be used. I needed at least eight metres to manage a vault and land on my hands. How on earth could they help?

Back in our rooms, Ryzia was playing with a makeshift doll—a wooden peg with a piece of rag tied around the middle. While I'd been outside, Mama had made our new lodgings more homey. The windows were now covered with the compulsory tar paper; the first room was to be our living and dining room, the second, our bedroom. It was now spread with straw mattresses and worn feather quilts. On the stove, a saucepan bubbled with soup. Admittedly, this was mostly water, turnips and potatoes, but with some hard black bread, it would fill our bellies.

When Papa and Adam returned, Adam's face was beaming. He unlatched a black case and held up its contents.

A violin!

Placing it under his chin, he produced a worn-looking bow and played a few notes. Though both needed new strings and the violin lots of tuning, I had never seen him so happy.

"Romek," Mama gasped. "Where did you find it?"

"Bought it from a musician in exchange for food."

"How sad for him," she murmured.

Sad for him, but happy for Adam.

"Yes. Pan Mandeltort used to play first violin with the Leipzig Orchestra. I have asked him to give Adam some lessons. We can only afford to pay him a few zlotys, but it means he won't starve."

As we settled at the table, Mama said, "Adam and Hannale, as soon as we finish eating, I have new clothes for you. Well, not new, they're second-hand, but I can alter them so they will fit."

"You will need them tomorrow," Papa added, smiling. "To wear to school."

"School? We're allowed to go to school?"

I never thought I would be so happy at the thought of going to school, but this was the best news yet.

Papa said, "There are some vocational schools, but strictly speaking you are not allowed to attend school. However, just like Panna Mislowski did, here teachers also run secret schools."

It seemed to me that in the ghetto our life was improving. What had I been so frightened of? We no longer needed to hide, Papa had a job and money. We had food and beds. And now I was going back to school.

I could hardly wait! Even better, there would be more books to read, not just *The Scarlet Pimpernel* or the tattered *Gazeta Zydowska*.

First thing the following morning, Papa led me and Adam downstairs and we walked three blocks to a house halfway along a narrow street. Once at the house, we had to climb three flights up to the school.

Near the entrance a small, elderly man seated behind a tiny desk introduced himself as Pan Rosenberg, the school principal. I wondered if he was as strict as my old headmistress before the war.

He told Papa how pleased he was that we were coming here and asked for our ages. When I told him I was almost thirteen, he tried not to look too surprised. He wrote our names and ages into a ledger and sent Adam in one direction, me in another.

Inside a room not much bigger than Mama and Papa's old bedroom was a small woman, her hair pulled into a bun, dressed in a neat if shabby blouse, cardigan and skirt, and thick wool stockings. Facing her were fifty students, all crammed into this tiny space.

She must have been told I was coming, because she said, "You must be Hanna Kaminsky. I am Panna Ranicki." She turned. "Everyone, please welcome our new student. Hanna, as you can see we are rather crowded, but I'm sure you'll find a space."

Because chairs were scarce, most students sat on the floor. I saw a vacant spot right down the back. As I wriggled into it, I felt everyone's eyes on me. Thankfully, Panna Ranicki was halfway through a lesson, and once I sat down she went back to it. "Can anyone tell me how many litres are in a kilolitre?"

A boy at the front put up his hand. "One thousand."

"And how many would be in a megalitre?" Panna Ranicki asked.

A girl just in front of me, answered. "One million."

"Thank you, Inka. And, Eva, could you tell me how many centimetres in a kilometre?"

"One hundred thousand, Panna Ranicki."

*Did I recognize that voice?* I stared at the back of the girl's fair hair. *Was it my Eva? My Eva, who was brilliant at arithmetic. My Eva whom I feared I'd never see again?*

She turned and gave me a huge smile.

Tears of joy filled my eyes. My best friend was still alive . . . and we were together again.

As soon as Panna Ranicki announced a break, we rushed toward each other to hug and kiss each other's cheeks. Our words tumbled over each other.

"I thought you were dead . . ."

"I was sure you were dead too . . ."

"When you didn't come back to school and we didn't know where you were, we hoped you'd escaped. Where did you go? What happened to you?"

I told her how I lost the silver rabbit she gave me, and when I found it again I was sure it was a sign that she was still alive. "I carry it everywhere."

Eva smiled and reached into her pocket. She pulled out the ivory elephant I had given her.

Eva told me how her family had also fled Warsaw, aiming for the Russian side of Poland. They had just made it outside the city when their car was stopped by German tanks. "They were going to shoot us," she said, her face crinkling at the memory. "We were as good as dead. Only Papa bribed an officer, and we came back. By then you'd already left. Where did you go?"

I told her about the farm and hiding in that loft and how the Germans took our animals.

"But why did your family come back to Warsaw?"

"Someone betrayed us. We don't know who for sure, one or other of the neighbours."

"And Elza . . . Where is Elza?"

I looked away and didn't answer. Eva immediately understood. She hugged me again, but this time her hug was full of sorrow for what we had all gone through.

Realizing some other girls were listening in, Eva turned to introduce me to her four friends. Inka was tall with striking cheekbones. Rosa had rosy lips, just as her name suggested. Everyone was very thin, Nina and Janette in particular. Eva told me that those two were inseparable. I thought each girl was beautiful in her own way, but in my mind no one could ever be as pretty as Eva.

Over the next few weeks, the girls became my friends too—although at first Rosa kept me at some distance. I think she had considered herself to be Eva's best friend and felt that I'd displaced her when I arrived. But I didn't want to worry about that. Being jealous of each other's friendships wouldn't help us survive.

Now back at school with all my friends, it almost felt like

our time in hiding was just some kind of bad dream. Even though living in the ghetto was a daily reminder of what we had lost, it also made me appreciate what was important.

I now realized going to school was to be valued as something precious rather than a chore. And there were new things to learn. Though Yiddish and Polish, and its hybrid YiddPol, were spoken in the ghetto, we studied Hebrew and English as well.

Papa insisting that we continue with our study of math and science while we were hiding meant I quickly caught up with those subjects.

Later, when I questioned Adam about this, he said it was the same for him.

My new friends loaned me lots of books to read. After so many years with only one, I wanted to consume an entire library.

Adam found happiness in his violin lessons. Papa paid Pan Mandeltort five zlotys each time. My young brother was extremely talented. Although, he was forbidden to play works by Jewish composers like Mendelssohn or Mahler, or by Chopin because he was Polish, or even Debussy because he married a Jewess, he was soon playing pieces by Mozart, Beethoven and Brahms. Still, hearing music and being with friends again seemed like a miracle after those two lonely years on the farm.

Once more life settled into a routine. Papa went to the Council early every morning. Adam and I walked together to school, while Mama and Ryzia stayed in our rooms, or occasionally went to the market. After school, we tended to stay indoors, since it was safest to be noticed as little as possible.

One afternoon, on the way home from school, Karol, Jacob and Moshe found me again. It had been a few weeks since I'd last seen them, and they seemed skinnier and dirtier than ever.

Jacob said, "Hanna, we got you a space if you still want it."

"Big enough for practise," Karol added.

Adam nudged me in the ribs. "What are they talking about?"

I ignored him. I was too anxious to find out if what the boys were saying could be true. I asked, "You sure? Where?"

Jacob said, "Weisman Hall. Big place. It's full of stuff . . ."

"But if we shove it away," Moshe butted in. "You got lotsa space."

"Only you hafta come with us right now."

"But I'm supposed to head straight home . . ."

"Have it your way, then." Karol shrugged and turned to walk away.

"No, stop!" I ran after him calling, "Thank you. Please show me."

"Follow us, then," he said, looking back over his shoulder.

I told Adam to head home. He was to tell Mama that I was with some friends and that I'd be back very soon.

I raced after the boys. For half-starved kids they were quick as jack rabbits. I was stronger than when I first arrived thanks to more food, but it was still hard keeping up—especially when I had to dodge my way around beggars and people streaming through the streets.

The boys stopped in front of a building. A sign said "Weisman Hall." I followed them through an unlocked side door.

On one side was a small stage, below that a larger area for the audience. But all chairs had been pushed against three walls, and that left enough space for me to practise my floor work. Of course there was no springboard for vaulting. No beam to balance on. No bars to hang from. No mats to soften a fall. But at least there was space.

"See?" Moshe said. "Told you."

"Show us what you can do," Jacob demanded.

I bit my lip before saying, "Uh, I haven't practised for years. I'll be hopeless."

"Don't matter." Squatting on the floor, each boy lit a cigarette and waited for me to begin. It flashed through my mind that they were too young to smoke. However, food and cigarettes were the ghetto's favoured currency.

I thought back to some of my old routines. During those years spent on the farm, I had gone over them so often in my mind, I could recall every movement.

Remembering was one thing. Doing them, another. Will my skinny, weakened body obey my mind?

First, I remembered to stretch very slowly, very carefully, so as not to pull any muscles. I plopped onto the floor and, using my hands for balance, tried some basic splits: those that had been drilled into me over and over again.

I glanced over at the boys. Puffing away like steam engines, their eyes stayed fixed on me as if I was some kind of unknown animal.

Back on my feet, I tried a few basic moves.

I ran, leapt and flung each leg behind me in turn.

The boys clapped and cheered.

Made slightly bolder by this small achievement, I tested myself further, tried a simple somersault followed by forward and backward bridges. Finally, I spun on one foot, then the other.

The boys clapped as if this was something spectacular.

I was so thrilled that I could still manage these moves, I decided to attempt an aerial cartwheel. That was a disaster. Instead of landing on both feet, I tripped, staggered and fell onto my knees.

Now out of breath and with two big bruises, I settled on the floor beside them murmuring, "I need lots more practise."

"So?" said Karol. "You got this place. Come here when you can."

I wondered why they wanted to help me. Wanting to know more about them, I leaned against the wall and asked, "Where do you live?"

Karol paused. "Here and there. Wherever we can find a place to squat."

"Not with your parents?"

"Nah. They're all dead," Moshe said flatly.

I stared at them, my heart welling with sympathy. These poor boys! Before, I had thought of them as just annoying street kids. Now I realized they were homeless orphans, forced to be resourceful. "What happened to them?"

"Mine were killed in the streets, here. Shot." Moshe's voice was still flat.

I was horrified. Of course I knew that the Germans were shooting us in the ghetto, sometimes randomly. They didn't care if we lived or died. They seemed to prefer us to be dead. The horror of what this meant hit me hard.

"Karol's parents were taken away," Moshe continued.

"Where?" I asked Karol.

Karol shrugged, but didn't look at me. "Last year they got taken. They took thousands off to labour camps. I suppose they're there, but I dunno where."

I turned to Jacob. The smallest of the three, he was surely the least able to cope on his own. "What about you?"

Tears fell down the boy's cheeks.

Karol said, "He lost his family on the way here. We think they're dead. But he's okay long as he stays with us." He jabbed Jacob's arm. "Right?"

Jacob nodded. Wiping his tears away he left dirty streaks on his cheeks.

Tears trickled down my cheeks, too.

I thought how kind it was of them to help me. But I did wonder what their reasons might be? What could they want that I might possibly give them?

Over the next few months, I went to the hall most days after school, while Adam went home with strict instructions not to dawdle or do anything to make himself obvious. Mama worried at first, but Papa convinced her saying, "Miriam, we can't allow the Nazis to take everything away. Let Hanna do what she loves."

Now that Papa was earning a small salary, he was able to buy more food with the help of the ghetto's smuggling trade. With the extra food, I was building up a lot of lost strength.

Sometimes, when I arrived at the hall, the chairs were pushed not against the wall, but set up for a performance that evening. Undeterred, I shoved them aside and when I finished, I returned them to their proper place.

One warm afternoon in July, I was halfway through a routine when a rear door opened. A middle-aged woman came over to where I was preparing to tackle a backward aerial somersault.

Hands on hips, like a teacher catching someone misbehaving, she barked, "This hall is my responsibility. No one gave you permission to be here. What's your name?"

"Hanna Kaminsky."

I tried to explain why I was here. She refused to listen. "You mustn't move these chairs once they've been set up. You're not to do it again, do you hear?"

"But no one's using this hall," I protested. "I'll move them back when I finish."

"Hmmph! Well, you're to put those chairs back right now and leave. Don't you dare turn up here without permission."

Anger and disappointment welled up. After returning the chairs I stormed home through the crowded streets to find Mama sitting on her mattress in our bedroom, reading a newspaper. It wasn't the *Gazeta Zydowska*, but one of the many illegal newspapers published in the ghetto that told us what was actually happening. Despite the risk, these underground newspapers were widely read.

"The Germans have attacked Russia," she announced to me.

"I thought the Russians were fighting *with* the Germans."

"Not any more. I think this is good news, Hanna. It is better to have the Russians on our side, and not against us. And I have some more good news," she went on. "I have been offered part-time work. Because of the huge numbers of Jews and gypsies coming in from the smaller cities and the countryside, the *Judenrat* needs more translators. I'll need you to look after Ryzia and keep an eye on Adam while I'm gone."

I eyed her warily. "When will that be?"

She paused before saying, "Afternoons, after school."

I felt myself redden. Before I could argue she went on, "Hanna, stop always thinking about yourself. Papa earns only enough to pay our rent and buy a little food. But everything is becoming more expensive. I know you want to continue your gymnastics, but given our situation, it's hardly a priority."

I knew Mama was right. Still, tears filled my eyes. Mama's words mingled with the words of the woman at the hall. I would never get to practise my gymnastics. Not ever again.

That night Papa came home with news of his own. "The Weisman Hall has been holding concerts to raise money for refugees."

Even in the ghetto, there were wonderful entertainment and cultural events. Music was performed by some of Europe's most celebrated Jewish musicians, there were exhibitions of paintings and sculptures, stories and poetry—many about life in the ghetto, were illegally published. There was a theatre on Nowolipki Street where ballets and operettas were performed, plus revues at the Femina Theatre with funny skits about the *Judenrat*.

Papa said, "It seems Weisman Hall has had such success they are running out of acts." He turned to me and Adam. "Today I was asked if my clever children might perform before a paying audience."

Mama looked pleased. "What a wonderful compliment. When?"

"In three weeks. Adam, do you think you will have something ready to perform?"

Adam raised the violin to his chin and started to play. Notes fluttered and danced through the air.

Papa smiled. "I guess that answers my question."

He turned to me. "What about you, Hannale? I know you have been practising your routines."

I gulped. "Maybe . . . But what if I'm not good enough yet? I've got no teacher to show me where I'm going wrong."

He came over to hug me. "Whatever you can manage will be perfect."

"But I won't have any chance to prepare before the concert. Mama wants me home after school to look after Ryzia."

"So come home, pick the little one up, and take her back with you to the hall."

Mama looked anxious. "Romek, you sure that's safe?"

He grimaced. "Darling, nothing is safe."

"There's another problem." I described what happened that afternoon with the woman at the hall.

"Not to worry, *bubbala*," Papa reassured me. "I'll clear things up with her."

"What about Adam? Mama wants me to keep an eye on him."

"I don't see any reason why Adam can't go to the hall with you and Ryzia. He can practise there too."

It seemed too good to be true. Once again, things had quickly changed, only this time for the better.

I felt so light-hearted I skipped downstairs to take the used bones that had been boiled for stock down to the garbage can in the back courtyard.

A boy sidled up to me. His face suggested he was about my age, maybe older, but he was shorter than me by a couple of inches. It was no longer possible to judge people's ages by their size. People had so little to eat, there was so much malnutrition, everyone seemed shorter, more stunted, than before the war.

He grabbed the garbage out of my hand saying, "I can do that for you."

"But I haven't any money."

"That's all right," he said quickly. "You can pay me with bread."

There were now so many homeless, orphaned children on the streets it was impossible to take care of them all. But he was so eager to work, and his eyes were so pleading that my heart melted. I thought of Karol and Jacob and Moshe and how they had helped me. How were we meant to survive under the German's deadly occupation and persecution if we didn't support each other?

What's your name?" I asked him.

"Janusch."

"Well, Janusch, come inside."

I took him upstairs to meet Mama. At first she was dismayed at how dirty and unkempt he was and she worried that he might carry some infection he would pass on to us. But there was something about him. His huge dark-brown eyes melted her heart as they had mine. She gave him his piece of bread and a bowl of soup. We told him he could sleep outside our door instead of on the street.

Janusch looked up at Mama. "You won't regret it, I promise. I can guard your rooms for you if you like."

Mama smiled. "That's very kind. Thank you, Janusch."

Mama started her new job the following day. After school, I came straight home with Adam to collect Ryzia and Adam's violin.

Mama was ready to leave. "Above all, children," she said

to us, "do be careful. Especially with Ryzia."

"Of course, Mama," I reassured her. "Don't worry."

Holding Ryzia's hand, her other clutching a peg doll, the three of us made our way to Weisman Hall.

I settled Ryzia in a corner of the stage where Adam and I could keep an eye on her. Adam began playing Mozart's Violin Concerto in A Major. I decided to practise on the stage too, as that was where I would perform.

Slowly stretching my back, neck and each limb so my body was ready to start moving without pulling a muscle, I began to think up a routine. Given the stage was smaller than the space I used in the past for a similar routine, I had to rethink everything. I tried a few flying leaps, followed those with a handstand, then some forward and backward somersaults. I stood on my hands with my legs scissoring, sprang back up to make a forward bridge, then tried a backward one.

I cartwheeled, attempting to land on the other side of the stage on both feet. That didn't work. There wasn't enough space. I needed moves that took place in one spot: moves like circling many times on one leg and circling on the other.

The stage floor dipped slightly toward the auditorium making balance more difficult. I kept falling over. Soon I was covered in bruises, but at least it kept Ryzia amused. She giggled each time I took a tumble. I did my best to ignore the aches and pains and start all over again. I had to make this appear effortless.

I remembered my old teacher saying that a good routine combined difficult tumbling skills with artistry, style and something she called "charisma." The more I thought about it, I decided "charisma" must be some quality that kept the audience's gaze riveted on the stage. It possibly had nothing to do with how many impressive moves I could make. Rather, it had to be something more, something indefinable, though right now I wasn't sure what that could be. Maybe it was just confidence?

There was still a final move to figure out, something that looked exciting without creating too much danger of falling and disgracing myself. I still had three weeks before I was to go on stage. I needed music to accompany this routine, I didn't want to ask Adam. He was busy getting ready for his own performance. Just below the stage was an upright piano. Mama was a terrific pianist. I had to talk her into accompanying me.

We were almost home when we were stopped by Karol, Jacob and Moshe.

"That your little sis?" Karol asked.

"Yes."

"*Shayne madel*," he said approvingly. *Pretty girl:*

Now nearly three, Ryzia's thick dark hair, large grey eyes with their abundant eyelashes, round cheeks and dimpled chin, hinted that one day she'd be beautiful.

Moshe said, "Hanna, we need your help."

"What kind of help?" I had been half expecting them to ask for something and here it was.

Karol glanced around before whispering, "Can't talk here. We hafta meet you a bit later."

"Curfew's at seven," I reminded him. "If we're caught on the streets, we'll be shot."

He shrugged. "We're out all the time. You jus' hafta stay invisible. Tonight real late, go to the courtyard at the back of your building. We'll find you there."

At first I backed away. Then I thought about it. Though I was nervous about breaking the curfew, I felt I owed them something. "All right, I'll be there." I promised. But all I could think was, *What could they possibly want of me?*

Mama and Papa were due home before the seven o'clock curfew. Mama had left turnips, potatoes, onions, beans and horse bones for me to cook. While we waited for them to come home, I peeled and chopped vegetables, tipped everything into a saucepan, added water and placed the pan on the stove. And while my hands were busy, I couldn't stop wondering what those boys had on their minds.

It was now well past seven. Adam was, as usual, engrossed in violin practice. Ryzia had fallen asleep on her mattress. My parents had still not come home and it was getting late.

I started to panic. What if the Germans had them? What if they had taken them the way they had taken Karol's parents —to slave in a labour camp who knows where? What if they'd been shot for being in the streets after curfew?

It was past nine o'clock when my parents did finally walk in, their faces grey with exhaustion.

I met them with a cry of relief.

"There have been more shootings on the streets," Papa said, grimly. "We had to hide until it was safe."

The soup was ready so we settled at the table. Because we had only four chairs, Ryzia sat on Mama's knee.

I asked, "How was work today, Mama?"

"I can't believe so many people are being sent into the ghetto," she slowly replied. "Mostly women and children. Where are the men?"

Papa stared at his plate as if the answer lay there. Then he looked up to say, "Some of the Jewish Militia are collaborating with the Nazis to send the men to work in German factories."

There was a long silence.

Papa broke it by asking me how the practice session had gone.

"I'm still working out a routine," I told him. "Only I can't think how to end it."

"You'll come up with something," he assured me.

I turned to Mama. "There's a piano. Will you play for me while I perform?"

Though Mama claimed her fingers had turned to

spaghetti, in the end she agreed. We spent the rest of the evening choosing music that might work, finally coming up with Bach's Prelude and Fugue in C sharp Minor.

Later, lying on my straw mattress, I forced myself to stay awake. Once I heard light snores coming from the other beds, I crept out of the room. Slowly I opened the door that led to the passage. It let out a horrid squeak. After checking no one was awake, I tiptoed to the back of the building and outside.

It was very dark. Only a fingernail of a moon could be seen through a thick layer of cloud. A light searching for enemy aerial bombers lit up the courtyard, then continued on.

"Hanna?" I recognized Karol's voice.

"Yes." I swallowed.

Someone whispered in the darkness, "We wanted to ask you if you could do your stuff."

I recognized Jacob's voice.

"What do you mean?" I whispered back.

"Your tumbling, that sorta thing. We need you to distract the guards."

The hair on the back of my neck stood up.

"You come with us and then do some of your stuff at the crossing of Sienna and Zelazna Streets, while we go through the sewers."

"The sewers?" My nose scrunched in disgust.

"We're smuggling in flour," Moshe said simply. "A baker is selling us sacks of flour. We gotta pick up the sacks and take them back to the ghetto. The kids in those refuge homes are starving."

Their suggestions scared me. Mama and Papa were always telling us not to draw attention to ourselves, and now these boys were asking me to do the exact opposite.

"The guards are sure to shoot me," I weakly protested.

"One guard is Polish. He's not so bad. We've bribed him to say you're his son and you're keepin' him company."

"How can I be his son when I'm a girl?"

"Those Germans are stupid. Just pretend. You're short and skinny. If you hide your hair, they won't see no difference."

I frowned. "I'll think about it and let you know."

"Don't think too long. If you can't help us, we'll hafta think of another way . . ." Karol said. "They need bread," he added almost as an afterthought. "Lotsa bread."

An image of a challah, a freshly baked egg bread, flashed into my mind. I could almost smell and taste that rich crisp crust.

"You mean, it's all for the kids in the refuge. You're getting nothing out of this?"

Moshe shrugged.

"When do you want to do it?"

"In a few days."

I swallowed, "It's far too dangerous. I don't think I can."

"I can show you something that'll change your mind?" Karol broke in.

Forgetting he couldn't see me in the dark, I nodded. But my heart thumped in my chest so loudly I was sure he could hear it. "All right."

"You hafta meet us tomorrow after school."

"I have to look after Ryzia."

"Bring her along. This'll be short."

I crept back into the building. Just as I was approaching our door, Janusch was beside me. "Heard all that," he whispered. "You gonna do it?"

"I don't know," I whispered back.

"If you do go, I'll come with you. You might need help."

"It's far too dangerous. You don't have to . . ."

Janusch shook his head. "Course I do. You helped me. My turn to help you."

The next afternoon, the gang met me and Adam and Ryzia as we headed for Weisman Hall.

"Come with us," Karol said.

"It's all right," I said to Adam. "You go ahead. I'll be there with Ryzia soon."

Adam looked at me doubtfully. "Don't be long."

"I won't. I promise."

Pushing our way through the crowds, Ryzia and I followed the boys around two blocks to the edge of the ghetto. They stopped in front of what might once have been a factory.

Karol beckoned us inside. The place was filled with small children, some lying on oil-stained floorboards, some sitting under torn rags and pieces of blanket. All had skinny arms and legs and hugely vacant eyes. Their bellies bulged due to starvation and malnutrition.

"They got no one to look after them," said Moshe. "An' they're too young to look after themselves. They need food."

I was too upset to say anything. A little voice inside my head began to drum two words over and over: "*pluck and audacity, pluck and audacity.*" I remembered those words from *The Scarlet Pimpernel* and how, stuck in the loft, I had wished I could do something more than feel sorry for myself. Now, in the ghetto, there was something more I could do.

I looked Karol straight in the eye.

"I'll try."

The next few nights my sleep was plagued with nightmares. The first night I dreamt of the start of the war and the endless bombing. In my dreams the falling shells whistled, the ground shook and buildings crumbled.

The following night, my dreams were of Zaida, Elza and Anya. They were almost close enough for me to touch, but I could never quite reach them. Then, looming large before me, blocking out all the sunlight, were German soldiers, the ones who killed Anya and Elza and took us away. I saw the faces of Andre and Jarek—either one of them might have been the person who turned us in to the Nazis. Their faces faded away to be replaced by the square, moustached face of Adolf Hitler, the German Führer so full of hate and false righteousness who started Europe's descent into war and murder.

When my eyes opened I was drenched in sweat. All I could do was wonder what those dreams were trying to tell me.

"Tonight," said Karol. "We're goin' tonight. Meet us at the back just before dawn."

"All right," I said, though my heart thumped in my chest. I only hoped I'd be brave enough to do what they expected. I felt confident that I could perform my routine. I had spent previous afternoons at the hall, going over it, starting with flying leaps, following them with a handstand and three forward and backward somersaults. Then I balanced on my hands, legs scissoring, springing back onto my feet to make forward and backward bridges. I finished this off by swivelling many times on my right leg; then the same on the left. That was it.

That night I was convinced I wouldn't wake in time. We had no clock and I had no watch. Almost no light came through the windows as they were blacked out with tar paper. I decided to do my best to stay awake so as not to miss the dawn.

At some point I did doze off, because I woke with a start.

When I thought it must be well into the early hours of the morning, I crept out of our rooms, down the corridors and the back to where the boys were waiting. Karol said darkly, "Thought you'd changed your mind."

"Not a bit," I whispered.

Another figure appeared out of the dark.

It was Janusch.

Karol turned. "What's he doing here?"

Janusch gestured at me. "Looking after her."

"Not this time," I said. "But thank you."

"Try to stop me," Janusch whispered, determined.

Karol shrugged. "All right, but make a sound and you're on you're own." He turned back to me. "You need to hide your hair."

I had already figured this out. I took Adam's woollen cap out of my pocket, pulled it on and tucked my hair inside.

"Right. Let's go."

I nodded.

But how were we to get to Sienna Street during the curfew hours without being shot?

I had underestimated the boys' resourcefulness. Instead of moving through the streets, their route involved climbing fences and criss-crossing backyards. We finally entered a bombed-out building where the boys led me through a tunnel dug under the house and into the dirt until we reached the ghetto wall. Janusch followed us in silence all the way.

At the base of the wall was a small opening for sewer pipes. By removing and replacing a few bricks, someone small, the size of a small child, could manage to wriggle through.

The ghetto wall rose many feet. Constructed from solid brick and concrete, it was topped by a thick layer of clay peppered with glass splinters intended to cut the hands of anyone trying to climb over. The gate that opened into the ghetto was just wide enough for a truck to pass through, and narrow enough for two guards to block.

At this morning hour, the guards seemed quite relaxed. They were dressed in their distinctive German helmets, warm woollen greatcoats and thick gloves. They sat smoking cigarettes, their bayonets propped beside them.

We peered out from a doorway in the shadows. Karol, Jacob and Moshe were tying burlap sacks around their middles. Their hands moved so efficiently, they had clearly done this before.

I whispered, "What do I do now?"

"See the guard on the left, the taller one?" Karol answered. "That's your Pole. You're to go over to him and greet him like you're his son."

In the dusty early dawn light, I could see the guard's face. How anyone could imagine we were related was beyond me.

He had flattened cheeks, pale protruding eyes and a mean small mouth.

"Won't the other guard wonder why I'm in the ghetto, and not on the other side of the wall?"

"Nah," said Jacob. "He's to tell the other guard you're running a message for him. They're expecting you."

This was it then. My tummy was full of butterflies wearing boots. But my fear had disappeared. What I felt was more like excitement. I felt a rush of adrenaline. I was no longer scared. Wasn't this just like the Scarlet Pimpernel? Like him, I had to fool the enemy.

Taking a deep breath, I stepped out of the doorway, and slowly made my way to the Polish guard.

"Good morning, Papa," I said, my voice gruff enough to sound like a boy's.

The guard turned, smiled and waved. Turning to the other, he said in broken German, "This is my son, Oskar. He is quite a useful fellow, aren't you, Oskar?

I nodded toward the German guard.

"Oh, yes, he runs messages for me. He's become my personal postman." The Polish guard gave a small laugh. "And he keeps us entertained. You'll see." He turned to face me. "Come, Oskar, show us what you can do."

"Of course, Papa."

There was just enough space to perform the routine I had practised so carefully. As I began, I could feel both guards' eyes fixed on me. I had to keep their attention as long as possible. Just in case I hadn't given the boys enough time, I repeated my routine, this time far more slowly.

"That's fine, son," the Polish guard said, as I finished. "Good work, that will do for now."

The German guard spoke to me.

"Yes, fine work. Why don't you head on home now with your papa?"

This was something we hadn't expected. I had to think quickly.

I looked at the Polish guard, hoping he would be able to help. "I still haven't had time to deliver the second message, Papa," I said.

My pretend father nodded at me and then turned to the German guard. "I'll have to wait for Oskar. You might as well go, there's nothing to do here. I'll wait for our replacements. Our relief is due anytime now."

It was starting to drizzle. The German guard looked up.

"If you're sure. Don't want to stay out in this weather if I don't have to."

Once he was out of sight, I waved to the Polish guard calling, "Thank you."

I headed back to where I hoped the boys were waiting for me. I found them carrying sacks of flour. I was speechless with admiration.

Moshe's arm was bleeding.

"Are you all right?"

"Caught it on some barbed wire on the way back. It'll be fine."

Karol pulled a filthy rag out of his pocket and pressed it against Moshe's arm. Perhaps the wound might have been better without that bandage, but I didn't dare interfere. They seemed to know what they were doing.

"How did it go?" Jacob asked me.

I felt a broad grin split my face. "I'm back aren't I? And so are you." For the first time in a very long time, I was proud of myself.

The day of the concert arrived. After performing for the guards, under fear of being shot if the truth was discovered, I had thought that performing in front of an appreciative audience should be easy. But I think my fear had worked in my favour in front of the ghetto wall. Now I was overcome with stage fright.

Adam was scheduled to play before me. The notes flew from his violin strings like melodious birds filling the hall. It seemed to me that in a world that still held such beauty, that maybe Zaida had been right, that justice must win out in the end. When Adam finished playing, the audience cheered and clapped like mad. I was incredibly pleased for him, but his success made my stomach heave more than ever.

"Don't worry, Hanna," Mama said comfortingly. "I'll be there too. If you're nervous, just look at me. Forget anyone else is there."

"*Pluck and audacity*," I murmured to myself. My heart slowly settled down to its normal pace. I no longer worried that I might disgrace myself. I knew I could do this.

My turn had come. Mama walked onto the stage first, heading to the piano. She was greeted with polite applause. I stood in the centre of the stage and looked out at the people below me. I saw a sea of faces. In the third row, I glimpsed the woman who'd caught me practising in the hall and thrown me out. To my astonishment, she smiled and waved.

I was ready.

Mama played the first few bars, and what remained of my stage fright disappeared entirely. As soon as I began, I was lost in the music and the movement, and my whole routine passed in a blur. I don't know how I managed it, but I do know that I didn't fall. When I landed on my feet at the end of the routine, I looked up to see Mama smiling, gesturing toward the audience.

The audience smiled and nodded. Clapped and cheered. I slowly realized they liked my performance. On the side of the hall I glimpsed Papa, standing up, beaming at me with pride. Ryzia, in his arms, was waving a tattered handkerchief and laughing.

I couldn't remember the last time I saw my family so happy.

Eating soup at our table in our rooms that night, Papa told us how much money the concert had raised for the refugees. He said, "Even in the midst of all the deprivation, we must still do what we can to take care of each other."

"I am so proud of you both," Mama said.

I wondered if I should confess to Mama and Papa what I had done with the boys. But they might think it too dangerous and stop me from doing it again. Because I had decided that I would.

Once again Janusch refused to be put off. He followed me down to the courtyard where I met the boys.

"All right," Karol said. "But this time you will have to make yourself useful."

"You bet," agreed Janusch.

I was no longer worried about the Polish guard. After last time, I felt I could trust him. This time he was with a different German guard. I didn't mind. It gave me the excuse to show off my routine to a new audience. I slowed it down as much as I could, even adding a few movements to make sure the boys had time to come back through the wall. Janusch was now on watch duty. He was to keep an eye on me and to call out if trouble was on its way.

But there was nothing he could do when trouble did arrive. The sun was up now, and the guard couldn't convince his companion to leave early. He no longer had the excuse of my staying behind and I was forced to follow my "father" out of the ghetto, alongside his German colleague.

On the other side of the wall, I walked into a totally different city . . . almost a totally different country. A tram trundled by. A cyclist rode past. Though one building further along the street had suffered from earlier bombings, there were very few signs of war. I could have been in a time warp. It was the Warsaw I remembered from 1939. I caught a whiff of frying sausages. Another unmistakable smell that could only be fresh baked bread. My mouth watered. But what astonished me most, was how empty this street was. How different it was to the crowded ghetto where it was barely possible to move without walking into someone. It was all so unbelievably, so incredibly, normal. It made what we were living through seem merely a bad dream, something from which we might hopefully wake.

The German guard took his leave, saying *"Auf weidersehn"* to my supposed Polish father. As soon as he was out of sight, I doubled back to where the sewer pipe ran through the wall. Thankfully, there were no guards on this side of the wall to see me.

I prayed that Janusch had let the boys know what had happened.

He had. Karol was waiting for me. "I thought this might happen," he said.

"Why didn't you warn me?"

"Would you have gone through with it if I had?"

He had brought an extra sack and I wrapped it around my body. Following him, I managed to wriggle back through the sewer and back into the ghetto.

Three weeks later, the boys asked me to play my role again. They had to wait until the Polish guard had a different guard sharing his shift at the gate. This gave me another chance to display my routine.

I felt less scared this time. Having crossed to the other side of the ghetto wall, we now had a plan to get me safely back. Now less might go wrong.

Or so we thought.

There was no sign of my Polish "father." Maybe he was sick? I had a sudden horrid thought that maybe his collaboration with us had been discovered.

Whatever the reason, two German soldiers blocked the entrance to the ghetto.

If I intended turning back, now it was far too late. The boys had already set off on their mission. They trusted that

I was confident enough to manage what I had to do. They needed me to distract those guards, otherwise they would be caught.

I shuddered and turned to Janusch. He had been so useful last time, we were all happy to have him here.

He whispered to me, "What are you going to do?"

"I have to do something," I murmured back. "But what?" The curfew was still in force and there was a great chance I would be shot for being out on the streets. I no longer had the protection of being the Polish guard's son.

"Sleepwalk!" Janusch hissed.

"What?"

"Pretend you're sleepwalking. Like you don't know what you're doing."

It wasn't a bad idea, though it did flit through my mind that there was no reason why those guards wouldn't kill me anyway.

I walked out of the doorway slowly, acting as if I didn't see them, hoping that they might be curious or amused enough not to shoot. After all, the streets were quiet, and they had probably spent a long, boring night.

One guard reached toward his holster.

He pulled out his gun.

The other guard laughed.

*"Pluck and audacity."* That voice was there again, helping me find my courage.

Pretending I was half mad, and as if I was on my way to a market, I muttered loud enough for those guards to hear, "Cabbage, onions, cabbage, onions."

The guard laughed loudly. "Silly Jew. He's got no idea where he is."

At least they believed I was a boy.

"It could be a trap," the other warned.

"A trap? Some skinny kid, walking in his sleep? My Joachim does it all the time."

"These Jews are cunning, remember?" The first guard's voice was malicious. "Don't forget why we've herded them in here."

I was terrified. But in order to keep distracting them, I kept muttering, "Cabbage, onions, cabbage, onions . . ."

I was at the street corner. Surely they would expect me to keep going if I really was a sleepwalker.

What now?

I turned and walked back toward the guards again. Still pretending not to see them, I murmured, "I forgot the box from Mama . . . cabbage, onions, cabbage, onions . . ."

"Go home, you stupid kid," the nastier guard yelled. "Go home before we shoot you!"

I started as if suddenly woken from a deep sleep and stared blankly at him.

His hand had moved back to his pistol.

He pulled it out and pointed it straight at me.

I darted across the street into the doorway where Janusch was hidden.

A shot rang out. It was followed by the acrid smell of cordite.

My ears rang from the whizzing sound of the bullet.

Just in time, just before he could fire again, Janusch pulled me further into the shadows. "You've been hit." He took off his shirt and pressed it against my shoulder. Only then did I see blood seeping down one arm. Pain immediately followed.

I was so frightened. Janusch did all he could to comfort me, saying, "It doesn't look too bad. But we need to stop the bleeding."

Karol, Moshe and Jacob appeared carrying full sacks, and looking pleased with themselves. Karol baulked when he saw Janusch leaning over me.

"What happened?

"Shot," I managed to squeak.

"Can you walk?"

"I think so. It's just my shoulder."

Jacob wasn't sure if it was best to wait until after curfew ended. Then I could walk through the streets without fear of being shot again. Or was it better to take a chance of return- ing through the back ways and tunnels?

"I'll chance it," I said, though I knew my shoulder would hurt, which it surely did.

As soon as I got home, I woke Mama and Papa.

"I don't know whether to be angry or proud," said Papa as

Mama fussed about me trying to clean the wound.

"I can't believe it," said Adam. "How long have you been part of the gang?" I could tell he was jealous, even though I'd been shot. "Do they need more help?"

Mama's hair just about stood on end. "Don't you even dare think about it," she cried glaring at him.

Papa went to look for a doctor he knew living on the ground floor of the next door building.

Doctor Robowski was small, totally bald and, though painfully thin, his skin had so many folds, it hinted he'd once been plump.

He examined my shoulder very carefully. In the end he said, "You were lucky. It's only a graze, though the wound is quite deep. Would have been a different matter entirely if the bullet had entered your body and stayed there."

He cleaned the wound a little more and bandaged it with strips Mama tore from a clean old rag. Then he placed my arm in a sling and told me to keep it that way until my shoulder healed.

That put an end to any gymnastics. At least for a while.

Mama and Papa made me swear I'd never try anything as dangerous again, even after I got better. Papa said, "I'll admit I'm impressed with you, *bubbala*. You have shown great selflessness and bravery, and I can't ask for more than that."

In the light of his praise, I felt myself redden.

But Papa hadn't finished. "Still, I am going to ask more of

you. Your life is precious, and we have already lost so much. We owe it to ourselves and to each other to stay alive. There are other ways you can help. Think of how you helped at the concert. When you are feeling better, perhaps you could perform again?"

I hugged him, but Papa's face fell. "More and more the Nazis seem to want us all dead. There's no pretending otherwise. Let's foil their plans a bit longer, eh?"

Mama squeezed my hand. "And remember, you stand a much better chance at helping others while you are alive."

"Yes, Mama. Yes, Papa. I promise."

By early December sleet and snow had turned the streets into ice skating rinks. The black ice was hard to see and it was only too easy to slip and fall. I had grown out of my only pair of boots. Water leaking through the cracks turned my toes to ice.

Soon it would be Chanukah, the Festival of Lights, and also Christmas. Though few Jews celebrated Christmas, before the war Mama and Papa had always set up a small tree surrounded with presents. They wanted to combine both festivals so we children didn't feel we were missing out. As Christmas went for only one day and Chanukah eight, we were lucky to have both.

Each day of Chanukah a new candle was lit on a special candelabrum called a menorah. We no longer had our menorah, and any candles we had were too precious to use in any other way. The ghetto was gloomy and dark, only lit by searchlights fingering the underside of clouds. It didn't feel festive at all. Mama was particularly upset. An edict had been issued that anyone owning a fur had to surrender it to the Germans. Her beautiful coat, though now shabby and tattered, had managed to make it with us to the ghetto. That coat had kept Ryzia from freezing these past two long, hard winters.

"They want our furs for the army," Papa told us. Working for the *Judenrat*, Papa was able to obtain more information that most people. "Since the Germans have turned on the Russians, they are now fighting in freezing conditions on the Russian front."

"I still can't believe the Germans were stupid enough to turn on their own allies. It serves them right. I hope they freeze to death!" It was rare to hear my gentle Mama vent such anger.

"A lot of them are," Papa replied. "And now they plan to use our furs to line their boots."

We spent New Year's Eve with the Lublinskis. They arrived before curfew and we shared what little food we had.

"What will this next year bring?" Aunt Zenia asked sadly. "I hardly dare wonder anymore.

"Peace, I pray," Uncle Harry said quickly.

"Let us toast to that, and to our loved ones, wherever they may be," Papa declared.

We had nothing to toast with, so we improvized with cups of weak tea. As we held up our cups, Papa's voice became solemn. "Tonight, we remember our family and friends." He looked at all of us in turn as he spoke. "We remember Zaida and my mother, gone so long ago. We remember Nanna and Zaida Goldberg, and hope that they remain safe in Paris. We remember our friends, both back at home and in the ghetto. We pray for Elza and Anya, and others who have died and hope they have found peace. We pray for those who have disappeared. We pray that we may see them again, and that they will live amongst us in health and happiness."

Papa's voice became choked. He had expressed what we all wanted to say, but in the midst of this war, I don't think any of us dared hope for this much.

"Amen," Uncle Harry said quickly.

"Amen," chorused Mama and Aunty Zenia.

"To 1942," Adam cried.

"1942," Ryzia echoed.

As distant bells rang out the old year, the flame in our lamp started to flicker. As the last bell tolled, the light went out with a crackle.

Undeterred, Uncle Harry started to sing "Lili Marlene." Adam joined in with his violin. The music was a great antidote for the previous sombre moments and Uncle Harry kept it up, following that song with "Night and Day" and "Begin the Beguine," which happened to be my all-time favourite. Our voices rose in the darkness, and Eva and I held hands and swung arms in time to the music. By the time we all fell asleep on our shared mattresses, we almost managed to forget the dismal world outside.

# 1942

That winter was particularly cold. Our only warming thought was that the United States had now entered the war.

Adam became tremendously excited by this news. He asked, "How quickly can the Americans beat Germany?"

Papa mused a moment before saying, "You'd think it would be fast, but Japan attacked them almost out of the blue, and then Hitler also declared war on them, too. The Americans will have to fight armies on both sides of the world."

"But it's better to have them as allies, isn't it?"

"Yes, indeed," Mama came in fervently. "We should pray that every day brings us closer to peace."

Adam straightened, soldier-like, to declare, "The Americans will lick Hitler into shape pretty soon. He's sure got it coming!"

But it was hard to keep our spirits up in the cold. The homeless huddled inside doorways or anywhere they could find shelter. What with the freezing conditions and lack of food, more and more people were dying. Staying alive was a struggle for everyone, and the homeless had little to no chance. I worried about the boys and wondered where they were spending their nights. I hadn't seen them in weeks.

Our ration of coke and coal we used to heat our rooms and cook with ran out in days. We wore everything we owned to stay warm. Before the war, on cold wintry days, we warmed our insides with Elza's hearty soups. She always had a treat for me when I got home from school. Just the memory made me feel a bit warmer. But then the tinge of too much sadness and loss set in.

I was sure I'd never see such food again. The food ration for Jews was only 184 calories per day—the equivalent of about two slices of bread. It was almost impossible to survive on so little. That all seemed to be part of the Germans' plan. Slow starvation was sure to get rid of us. The non-Jewish Poles received 700 calories, which still wasn't much. Soldiers were allowed 2,500 calories. I suppose that made it more tempting for them to join the army. Though their lives were in more danger, at least they got fed.

Mama and Papa's earnings at the *Judenrat* kept us from the point of starvation—we could buy food on the black market, usually potatoes. These potatoes had been meant for German soldiers fighting in Russia. Since that country was so cold, the vegetables froze and then were sent back to us. We knew rotten potatoes could be poisonous, so first we boiled them before frying them as pancakes. We also ate little fish, everyone called "stinkies," that came in cans and tasted like salted herring. There was bread, but it was scarce. Even though Karol, Jacob and Moshe and other children some as young as four, smuggled grain through the wall, there was never enough to go around. Bakers were forced to buy grain from the collaborators at inflated prices. In turn they charged more for each loaf.

I hated the collaborators almost as much as I hated the Germans. They were the only ones living as richly as they had before the war. People gossiped that they lived on steak and champagne. All we knew was that they were fat and healthy, while we were painfully thin and sickly.

I had to give up my gymnastics. I had become too weak to manage cartwheels, one-legged twists and somersaults. Mama told me I couldn't afford to waste what little energy I had on exercise. Besides, there wasn't much space in which to practise now. These days, many concerts, plays, films and readings were held in Weisman Hall. Our creativity was the one thing the Nazis couldn't take away.

Given Jews were among some of the finest musicians in Europe, we had a splendid symphony orchestra. They were so good, some of the German soldiers on patrol used to stop at the back of the hall to listen. Adam's violin teacher had persuaded the orchestra to allow him to become part of the first violin section.

Adam was desperate to join. "Can I?"

Mama wasn't sure. "The children are weak with lack of proper food and proper vitamins, Romek. We have nothing left to fight off any diseases. It would be the end of us."

She was even anxious about us going to school.

Papa didn't agree. "They must continue their studies, Miriam. We can't give up yet."

Our classroom was less crowded now. Nina and Janette had died last November. They had stood little chance of making it through the dreadful winter conditions, they had been so thin and malnourished. Several of the younger children no longer turned up. I wasn't sure what had happened to them. Eva and I didn't dare ask. The best we could do was steel ourselves and do everything we could to stay alive. I didn't want my heart to grow cold, but it was too exhausting to grieve for everyone we no longer saw. There were too many to mourn.

Rosa's older sister died from typhus in January.

Rosa also stopped coming.

I asked Eva, "Do you know if she's all right?"

Eva shook her head. "I haven't heard. Mama won't let me go to see her."

"Me neither," I had to admit. "Even Papa is getting nervous about illness and he's usually so stoical."

The following Tuesday, both Eva and Alex weren't at school. Adam looked at me, frightened. I went to Panna

Ranicki to ask, "Have you heard anything, Panna?" I wasn't sure I wanted to hear the answer.

She shook her head. "No, Hanna, but no doubt we will see them both tomorrow." She did her best to sound reassuring, but it didn't quite work.

Eva and Alex didn't turn up the next day either. I was too upset to concentrate on any work, and as soon as I got home I asked Mama if I could visit her.

"Sit down, Hanna, Adam," Mama said softly. "We got the news today that Uncle Harry has died."

A lump caught in my throat, the lump so large I thought it might suffocate me.

"And Eva?"

Adam clutched my hand. Tears rolled down his cheeks.

"Aunty Zenia is doing the best she can," Mama told us. "She's well enough for now. But it's very hard for them."

I couldn't believe that cheerful, kind Uncle Harry was dead. He had always seemed larger than life. And now he was gone.

I couldn't stop fretting and worrying about Eva. Adam took refuge in his violin. His music was slow and mournful. Papa would plead with him to stop, to come to talk with him or to play with Ryzia, but Adam would hold onto his violin like it was life itself.

Then the news came that Alex had died. He had become more and more ill until there was no longer any hope. Thankfully, Eva seemed to be recovering.

Mama cried. "We must pray for her and for Aunty Zenia. What they must be going through!"

Ryzia went over to Mama and placed her little arms around Mama's neck.

Mama held her close saying, "We can only pray to God that he continues to spare us."

It was two weeks before Papa finally allowed me to visit Eva and Aunty Zenia.

To get there, I had to cross the two-storey bridge over Leszno Street. Aunty Zenia must have been listening out for me because I found her in the hallway outside their room. Her face was gaunt and I wondered if she had the strength to look after Eva, especially after losing her husband and son. She must have guessed my thoughts because she whispered, "Don't worry, Hanna. I won't let Eva die, I promise.

I hugged her in silence. What could I say?

I found Eva lying on her straw mattress. Her thick lovely hair had been shaved off and her skin was so pale, I hardly recognized her.

Mama had made me promise not to touch her, but as soon as she realized I was beside her, we fell into each other's arms.

For a long while she couldn't stop sobbing. She kept

repeating how much she missed her father and brother. There was nothing I could do to console her, nothing other than listen.

"Just seeing you again helps." She managed a weak smile. "Tell me about school. What have you been studying?"

"Loads of English, so we will be ready when the Americans beat Hitler now that Germany has declared war on them too. You know I think these Germans are quite, quite mad."

Eva managed to prop herself up before saying, "Now the Japanese and the Germans have united, they intend to conquer the whole world."

"I don't know much about the Japanese, but I do know what happened to Germany after the Americans joined the last war."

"What about the Russians?"

I shook my head in mock despair. "I still can't believe the Germans declared war on their own ally."

"Me either." She gave me a tiny smile.

"Well," I said firmly. "I'd much rather have everyone on our side than the other way around. But now I don't know who is left for Germany to declare war on. Maybe Switzerland?"

We managed another watery laugh.

"Everyone at school is missing you so much," I told her. "They keep sending their love and asking me how you are."

"They can't miss me as much as I miss them. Please tell Panna Ranicki I will be back soon."

Aunty Zenia came back into the room. "She's getting tired now, Hanna. And it's getting close to curfew time. You'd best head for home."

"I'll come back soon as I can." I squeezed Eva's hand. "Promise."

I made my way back to our apartment. When I got in, Mama was lying on the mattress, her eyes closed. Ryzia was on the floor playing with her favourite peg doll and a rabbit Mama had made from old socks too ragged to be darned. I thought back to the shelves stuffed with toys when I was Ryzia's age and ached for her.

It was unusual for Mama to be lying down during the day. Anxious, I asked. "Mama, you okay?"

"I'm fine." She opened her eyes. "Yes, just a bit tired."

She looked her usual self, no flushed cheeks or fever. But I worried now more than ever before. We had to do our best to stay healthy.

We didn't see as much of Janusch as we used to. He still sometimes slept across the doorway to our apartment and would come inside to play with Ryzia. I assumed he was helping Karol and the others smuggle grain through the wall, but he never said anything. I guess he didn't want me to worry. He seemed to regard himself as my protector. I had a lot to be grateful to him for. I had spoken to the boys once or twice since I was shot, but they realized that I could no longer help them. They were so resourceful I felt sure they would manage without me, just as they had before.

If Papa had a bit of spare money, he would take Janusch with us to concerts and plays at Weisman Hall, and he usually sat between me and Adam.

One day I found him sitting cross-legged in the passageway with a notebook and stub of a pencil.

"What are you writing?" I asked.

"A play." His face beamed with pride. "Do you want to read it?"

I did.

Though Janusch could have done with some spelling lessons, he had a natural ear for dialogue. His play was set in the ghetto, just like many of the plays we had seen at the Hall. However in Janusch's play the Americans rescued us. His American soldiers were like a posse of cowboys from the Wild West. One was even called Billy the Kid.

"This is wonderful, Janusch," I told him. I promised to help fix his spelling and then send it to one of the underground newspapers.

His eyes widened with pleasure. "Do you think they'd want to print it?"

"Yes, I do," I assured him. "And they'd be lucky to have it. For someone who doesn't go to school, you've got lots of talent."

Papa had been trying to convince Janusch to go to one of the new religious schools that had been recently set up.

"The Germans had allowed schools to be run in the ghetto and they received funding from the *Judenrat* and were able to expand. Previously all schools had been hidden or disguised as something else, like a soup kitchen or medical centre.

Papa suggested that I might want to change schools, but I liked Panna Ranicki too much to want to leave. Janusch was keen to improve his English. But those new schools concentrated mainly on religion, and that didn't interest me.

One day a girl called Maria joined our class.

She had wide-set blue eyes, very straight hair that was so blonde it was almost white, and a soft rosebud mouth. She looked so typically Aryan, only her longish nose hinted at any Jewishness. She was tall and healthy. I wondered what she was doing here?

She settled at the back of the room, her face expressionless, and did her best to make herself invisible, answering any questions only in whispers.

Inka sidled up to Maria after the lessons ended and introduced herself and me.

"Have you just arrived?" Inka asked. "I mean, to the ghetto?"

"It's all an awful, awful mistake," Maria whispered. Her pink cheeks turned redder.

"What do you mean?" I asked.

"It's a punishment."

"We are all being punished," Inka said. "But not for anything we've done. We're punished because we're Jewish."

Maria suddenly found her voice. "But I'm not Jewish. My father is . . . was . . . an official of the Nazi party."

I took an involuntary step backwards.

"Then why are you here?"

"They killed my father. He'd done something wrong. I don't know what. I don't believe he did anything wrong at all."

"But why would they send you, his daughter, to the Jewish ghetto, even if he had done something wrong?" Inka persisted. "I don't understand."

"My great-grandmother was Jewish, but when she married my great-grandfather, she converted. Mother only told me after Father was shot. But you know what . . ." She gave a loud sob, "I still don't understand how that makes me Jewish?"

"That's because being Jewish comes down the female line," I said. "It means your grandmother, your mother, and you are definitely Jewish, no matter how much you might hate it."

"Is your mother in the ghetto with you?" Inka did her best to sound kind.

"Yes. The two of us are here. We didn't know a soul when we got here. We couldn't find anywhere to live."

"Have you now?"

"We're sharing with another family. Mother had a little money that she sewed into the hem of her dress for emergencies. It's all we've got left." Maria stared at her feet as if she'd never seen them before.

For a moment I had a horrible thought: that it served her right. I felt a mean thrill to see an "Aryan blonde" come down in the world. Then I checked myself. We'd all come down in the world from our comfortable lives. And Maria couldn't help being blonde-haired and blue-eyed. She couldn't help having a Nazi-officer father any more than I could help being the child of my own parents.

It was harder for Maria. At least we all had each other. She and her mother must have felt very alone and isolated, even in this crowded ghetto.

"Mother said this morning if only we could go to church. She always felt comforted there."

"Actually, she can," Inka said. "There's a church for converts on Zelazna Street."

Maria was so grateful to hear this, she thanked Inka over and over, saying, "You don't know how much this means to me!"

That night I told Papa her story. "She told us she wanted to become a nun." I took a deep breath. "You know, I couldn't think of anything worse than locking myself away in a convent. And aren't we going through enough poverty and obedience to last us a lifetime?"

Papa nodded. "Your friend is fortunate to have such strong beliefs. Faith, regardless of what kind, sustains many people through dreadful trials."

On Monday, Maria told Eva and me that she had gone to Mass with her mother. "Mother sends you her thanks. It's really lifted her spirits."

I was curious enough to ask, "Did it make you feel better too?"

She shyly nodded.

Most Saturdays I continued visiting Eva who, thankfully, was starting to recover, more colour returning to her cheeks. One Saturday I found her out of bed seated on a chair propped up by cushions. When I asked where the cushions had come from, she said, "Mama asked the *Judenrat* for help."

This surprised me. "I didn't think they had any money. They keep trying to raise funds."

Eva nodded. "Yes, we have to return them when I get better, though . . ." she sighed. "Right now, I feel as if I never will."

"Course you will," I said. Though she was still so thin and wan, her scalp covered in wisps only starting to grow back, I wished I could really believe this.

That evening, Adam was performing in a "Young Artist" event. Papa and Mama had relented and let Adam perform.

He had been practising for hours but it always seemed he didn't need to. He truly was the child prodigy Pan Schmidt had always claimed he was.

The concert was a raging success. Adam was the last to perform, and I thought the other artists, all older than him, were pretty good, too. A girl with dark frizzy hair played a Beethoven piano sonata. Another, a skinny tall girl, sang a Schubert song in a lilting soprano and a boy, I guessed him to be about eighteen, played the Saint-Saen Cello Sonata.

When it was Adam's turn, I was terribly nervous in case he made a mistake. Then I told myself he wouldn't. Mama accompanying him on the piano, he performed the slow movement of a Mozart violin concerto. As I listened to his music fill the hall once more I wondered how, in a world that still held such beauty, could such evil and cruelty exist?

"There has always been good and evil," Papa whispered, as if he read my mind. "Ever since the garden of Eden. Remember it is our choices that make the difference."

The ghetto was shrinking and the population diminishing. Over the past few months nearly one hundred thousand people had died as a result of disease, starvation, random killings and the intense cold.

The Germans continued to reduce the ghetto walls to what they called the "Central Ghetto" or "Little Ghetto." With so many people crammed together, life became stifling. The Nazis had begun mass deportations to the Treblinka Labour Camp. This lessened the population of the ghetto, yet we remained like rats trapped in a cage rapidly becoming too small to contain us.

Mama was becoming more and more silent. These days she rarely spoke, not even to Papa and us children. Papa and I knew she was becoming deeply depressed. It didn't help her low mood that she was now busy processing Jews from Danzig who were being brought into the ghetto before being sent on to labour camps. The inhabitants of Danzig had lived as a free people since the last war, neither under German nor Polish rule. But the Nazis had attacked Danzig along with Poland in September 1939.

Papa said that Mama's sadness came from hearing dreadful stories about atrocities being committed in that city. Those that still survived now faced the prospect of more cruelty, and a future of forced labour and starvation.

"She thinks death would be kinder to them," Papa explained to me. He sighed deeply. "Sometimes I wonder if she is right."

We relied on Papa to keep us going, to keep our spirits lifted in this darkness. If both Mama and Papa fell into despair, what would become of us children?

As a result of the sadness around me I often felt empty, as if all could do was wait for the inevitable. Was there to be no rescue from this horrible situation? Would our only way out be through death? *"Pluck and audacity."* Those words from *The Scarlet Pimpernel* that I had clung to all these years now rang hollow in my mind.

In an effort to lift our spirits, Papa spent precious zlotys on a gramophone and some records he found in one of the markets. One record had Otto Klemperer conducting Beethoven's Ninth Symphony—music that promised better, fairer times. As we sat around the gramophone listening to the orchestra and chorus perform the "Ode to Joy," Papa said, "Amazing to think how Klemperer could side with the Nazis, yet still produce such wonderful music."

It had taken Eva several months to be well enough to return to school. Her hair had grown long enough to be shaped into a bob that really suited her. Even though she was so thin and pale, I thought her just as pretty as before. The boys who still turned up to school thought so too, because they clustered around her. Knowing how sick she had been, they kept offering to do small tasks, and she was always given the room's most comfortable chair.

As time went on more of my classmates simply disappeared. Maria stopped coming. Then Inka. I couldn't imagine why our family had been spared so far.

But every time I started to think this way, Papa would remind me, "We can't afford to give up hope. Not when hope is the only weapon we have. The way we fight back is by surviving."

I looked up at his dear face, a face that had once been so round and was now so shrunken; at his bushy beard, once quite black and now completely white. Both my parents looked decades older than they really were. Both had white hair and wrinkles as if they had aged twenty years in only four.

The following day, as often happened, an SS officer armed with a stick hit anyone who walked down Leszno Street on their way through the Little Ghetto. Many people had blood running down their faces. I remembered Papa's words, but I was finding it harder and harder to hold on to hope, when our reality was so randomly brutal.

Despite Papa's wise words, and our best intentions, all of us were falling under a black cloud of depression. Mama was working hard, but her work was taking its toll on her energy and her spirits. She saw and knew too much. Adam became more and more horrified by the injustices around us, he could no longer lose himself in his music. He refused to take any interest in his violin. Whenever Papa suggested he play for us, he shook his head. Adam, who had always been so easy-going, started to bicker about little things. So much so, to avoid any arguments, Ryzia and I spoke to him as little as possible. I felt sorry for him though. He had lost Alex, where I still had my best friend. The thought of losing Eva was so terrible, I could understand why he was so angry.

Poor Ryzia was outgrowing her dolls, and where a child her age would usually be exploring the world, she was cooped up. She had started to curl into a corner, soothing herself by sucking her thumb and rocking. I found myself retreating to the opposite corner at times when I was too miserable to do any homework or even read. Instead I bit my nails until the tips of my fingers bled—at least the pain reminded me that I could still feel.

One Saturday, when I was moping in my corner, Papa looked across at me from the table where he was reading one of the underground newspapers. "Hanna, why not offer your help to a school? One has just started across the road from here."

The schools were always asking for volunteers.

"There aren't any schools on Shabbat."

"Yes, there are. And most of the students have no one to look after them. It is up to more lucky ones like us to be responsible for their wellbeing."

"Lucky?" My heart was full of misery. But not wanting to contradict Papa, I said, "If you think so, Papa."

I told Eva about it and she agreed to come with me.

The school was situated in a cellar in a building that had once been smart, but certainly wasn't any longer.

Most of the children were very young, many no more than three or four. They jumped up when they saw us, clustering around us and asking for food. Mama had been able to find us some sweets. They weren't very nice, a mix of saccharin and molasses that the ghetto chemists produced, but they were like manna from heaven for these starving children. I couldn't remember the last time I had seen such joy.

Their teachers introduced themselves as Dorishka and Anna. We played Tiggy and Hide and Seek and Jumping up and Down and then, laughing, sat on the floor to sing in Yiddish, "Raisins and Almonds," "With a Needle," and the "Song of the Baker Boy."

Our singing over, and our voices so croaky, Dorishka called a break. The children went to play with the few toys that had been salvaged for them, and Eva and I joined the teachers in having a glass of hot water sweetened with saccharin as there were no tea leaves.

Before the war both women had been teachers. "Look at these kids," Anna said sadly. "Without parents, what chance do they have?"

"What chance do any of us have?" Dorishka was filled with bitterness. "But we have to keep living, we have to keep trying to survive . . ." her voice trailed away and she looked into space.

"Dorishka's husband has disappeared," Anna explained. "We haven't seen or heard of him for over a fortnight,"

"All those people are being shipped to the Treblinka Labour Camp, I can only imagine that he's ended up there."

Eva asked, "Do you know what happens in that camp?"

Dorishka shook her head. "No one has ever come back to tell us. The Germans claim they are being sent to work in their factories, but . . ." she hesitated. "I'm not sure if this is true. Who can you believe?"

"Certainly no Nazi," I said grimly.

"You know, before the war I had so many gentile friends," Anna mused. "Surely there must be some left who see what is happening and are trying to stop it."

"There is the Polish Resistance," Dorishka reminded her.

"What's that?" I asked, my ears pricking up.

"It's called the Polish Underground State. They are loyal to the old Polish government."

"How do you know?" I asked.

Anna smiled grimly. "My husband was in the Polish army but escaped before the surrender in 1939. He's been fighting for Poland ever since as part of the resistance movement. He is now in the *Armia Krajowa*, the Home Army."

"How many of them are there?" I couldn't believe I was hearing this.

"I don't know, but by now there must be tens of thousands, maybe even over one hundred thousand?"

"That many!" gasped Eva. "If your husband is in the Home Army, does that mean there are other Jews as well?"

"Some," Anna told us. "But most Jews who have managed to escape the ghetto are hiding in the forests and have formed their own partisan resistance movement."

"That's wonderful!" Eva cried.

"I'm not sure I'd call it wonderful." Anna was very matter of fact. "They don't have much in the way of weapons and if they're caught, they're tortured and shot."

Still, this was the most heartening news I'd heard in a long time. I couldn't wait to go home and tell my family. I was sure this would lift their spirits. Even Mama's.

Returning home I found Adam talking with Janusch at the table. Both boys' eyes lit up when I repeated what Anna and Dorishka had told me. I hadn't seen a look like that from Adam since Alex had died.

"I've heard a few whispers about the resistance," Janusch said. "Not much."

"Where?" Adam asked.

Janusch shrugged. "Here and there."

"Well, I know very little, but this is news worth celebrating," Papa declared. He set off for one of the bakeries in

Nowolipki Street at the edge of the Little Ghetto. He told us he would buy the best bread he could lay his hands on.

Just the thought of that bread made my mouth water. I had learned to live with hunger, but some days were worse than others. Sometimes that aching, empty gnawing in my belly meant I could barely think of anything else.

Mama turned on the stove, using the smallest amount of coal she could, to heat up the remains of the stew she had made.

"We won't touch it until Papa comes home, that won't be long," she said. "But we can enjoy the smell. That will be enough for now."

An hour went by, then two. By now Mama was beside herself with worry. "Something's wrong," she kept muttering over and over.

"He might have been forced to hide and wait somewhere, Mama," Adam said. "You know that happens to all of us often enough."

"I'll go," I said.

"We'll both go!" Mama was suddenly forceful.

Leaving Adam and Janusch with strict instructions to look after Ryzia and not open the door to anyone apart from us, Mama and I pulled on our threadbare coats and set off.

We arrived outside the bakery a short time after, without running into any problems. But once we arrived, it was obvious what had happened.

I was used to awful sights, even the sight of dead bodies in the street. There was so much death in the ghetto every day, people dying from starvation, cold, disease. And many others who were the victim of brutal, random shootings by Nazi soldiers.

On the ground outside the bakery were the dark shapes of about thirty crumpled bodies.

A man was bent over the body of an elderly woman, gently cradling her head. He looked up at us.

"They shot all of them," he sobbed. "They were just waiting to buy bread."

Mama stood like a statue, her face still and expressionless.

The man sobbed and then shook his fist violently.

I couldn't speak. I walked down the length of the queue of bodies, looking for my father. I found him, right near the door of the bakery. His arm lay protectively over a woman lying next to him, as if he had attempted to shield her, even as they both faced certain death. His face showed no signs of his last moments of terror, and I could see a small, round bullet wound in the centre of his forehead. In my grief I found enough strength to be grateful that he must have died instantly, that he didn't suffer.

I knelt beside him, and took hold of his hand, weeping silently, saying goodbye to my poor, dear, wise, kind Papa.

# 1943

What little core of resistance Mama still had disappeared entirely after Papa's death. She went to bed, closed her eyes and stayed there for days. I tried to get her to drink and eat a little, but it was useless. Without Papa, she had lost any interest in surviving.

Ryzia was only just four years old. Adam and I knew that if Mama wasn't able to take care of her, we would have to do so instead.

We decided to take turns staying home and going to school. Going there was becoming even more dangerous ,as the Nazis had begun raiding some schools and taking children away.

Without Papa, we no longer had any money coming in. Mama also stopped going to work. She was no longer capable of doing anything except lie on her mattress, eyes closed. After a week she had got up, but we couldn't get her to leave our room. She still resisted eating, but I persuaded her to take a bite. If I insisted that she eat more, she would turn her head away from me.

Papa had hidden a few zlotys under his mattress. If I was very careful, that money might last us a few more weeks. What we would do after that, I had no idea.

Even if we had enough money, food was becoming harder to find. I spent hours combing the ghetto trying to sift out something, anything. After some days I found a shop selling a strange grain that looked more like chaff. I decided it would have to do.

Totally despondent, walking head down, I heard gunfire just ahead. This was not unusual, but since Papa's death I'd become more and more afraid. I ducked into the first doorway I saw and watched the German truck drive off. I didn't want to think what horrendous sight lay around the corner.

I stepped out of the doorway, straight into a German soldier. I collapsed onto the ground, too terrified to move. What would be the point? I knew that I was about to die.

I closed my eyes and waited. All I could think was *who will look after the others?*

When nothing happened, I opened my eyes and found the young soldier staring at me. For an endless moment, we just looked at each other. His uniform—a metal helmet, a warm coat with a velvet collar, thigh high boots, and a baton and gun dangling from his belt—was impeccable. He was as long and thin as a pulled out noodle. His face was also long and pale, his eyes a watery blue magnified by thick glasses. I had never seen anyone look so unsuited to soldiering.

He reached out a tentative hand, as if to help me up.

I shrank back.

"Don't be scared," he said in German, then he repeated it in halting Polish. "I won't hurt you. Promise."

If I was too frightened to speak, my face must have shown disbelief.

"It is horrible here," he whispered. "What is happening to you . . . to your people . . ."

His eyes reddened and filled.

I was so startled I could only nod.

He pulled me up, and with his hand on my back guided me to a nearby alley where we couldn't be seen from the street.

I still didn't dare trust him. I didn't know what he was planning to do with me.

He began speaking quickly, darting glances this way and that, whispering in a hoarse voice, "Please, can I talk to you?"

What could I do but nod? I was sure he was crazy. I was far too scared to utter a sound.

"You understand German?"

I tried to say "*Ja*." The word stuck in my throat. I cleared it and nodded.

He sighed with relief, saying, "When this war began, I was only a student, I was studying theology . . . religion. I was going to be a priest. You understand?"

"*Ja*," I managed. "*Naturlich*."

"I'm no Nazi. They are evil. I hate them with all my heart."

I looked at him blankly.

"I don't want to be in their war. I was conscripted last year. I'm not much use as a soldier to them. As you see, my eyesight is dreadful. So they sent me here. Into this hell. I can't witness this without saying something. But what can I do?"

"What do you want from me?"

Nothing, nothing," he said. "Only to talk to you."

"You want to be my friend?" I asked in disbelief. Anger burnt at the back of my throat. "How can I be that?" I whispered fiercely. "You've gone along with it, haven't you? What have you done to try and stop it?"

He took off his glasses and blinked at me short-sightedly. "What can I do? I'm as caught as you are in the hell. Equally powerless. There are many of us back home that also hate Hitler and his henchmen. But if I, if *we* dare protest, we are sent to prison or shot."

I knew that what he was saying was true. So far I had kept myself alive while my entire world was being destroyed. If I didn't hold to who I knew was my friend and who was foe, how could I ever hope to survive?

He shook his head. "This world is so removed from any kind of humanity. We are all in terrible danger, no matter what side of the wall we are on. No one will ever be free of what is happening here."

He reached into his pocket and took out a handful of notes. "Take it."

I shook my head. If I took his money, he would see it as an act of forgiveness, and I didn't know how I felt about that.

"Don't be foolish," he insisted. "It's all I can do. Please let me help you."

I needed the money for Ryzia and Adam. There was no point in surviving this long and then dying from pride. I took the money and ran. I didn't thank him. But the soldier had given me a lot to think about.

It had never occurred to me that many Germans might be as unhappy as we were. So many of us, on both sides of the war, were victims of Hitler's vision of evil. Elza and Anya had paid the ultimate price when they could have chosen not to risk their lives. This sad, desperate German soldier had made a choice too. He tried, in the only way within his power, to show kindness. I realized that not everyone on the other side was our enemy.

Despite my hunger and fear, knowing this—and knowing that there was a resistance movement, Jewish partisans and the Home Army, who were all doing their best to fight against this new world of destruction—gave me a little bit of strength.

I could only hope it would be enough.

When I got home, Adam was waiting for me in the passage. He was crouched down with Ryzia, who was playing listlessly with her peg doll.

Adam whispered, "Mama." He didn't need to say anything else. I understood.

"It happened so quickly," he said. His face was expressionless. He must have felt as numb as I did.

"There was no warning." Adam's words suddenly tumbled out in a rush. "She said she had a sore throat, her cheeks were red and she got hotter and hotter. She kept throwing off her blanket and muttering. About cake. Oh I don't know what she was saying! She hadn't eaten for so long and she was so weak." Adam paused for breath, but just for a moment.

"I tried to put the blanket on her, it was freezing outside, and Ryzia tried to soothe her. There was no doctor to find, too many people have gone or have been taken away. And now Mama!" Adam started sobbing now, big huge gulping sobs.

Ryzia looked up at me silently. I picked her up.

She was so hot . . . far too hot.

"Adam! She's burning up!"

We took her inside the room, where I sponged her face and neck with a wet cloth to bring her temperature down.

I sang to her the song Mama always sang to her. She tossed and turned, sweat pouring off her little body. I'd stroke her hair, but she'd push my hand away and then reach out to grab it again.

Eventually she fell asleep, exhausted.

I told Adam to sleep too.

I couldn't shut my eyes. Every time I did, images of Mama and Papa, Zaida and Elza broke my heart into pieces.

I watched my brother and sister sleep until the grey light of dawn came through a crack in the blacked-out window.

That morning, only Adam woke. Our sister was dead.

There was no one left to mourn Mama's and Ryzia's deaths except me and Adam and Janusch. Together we carried their seemingly weightless bodies out to the street. There we waited for the cart that would take them to Cmentarz Zydowski to be buried in a mass grave.

"It will be our turn next," Adam said miserably. "We have no money, no food. How can we possibly survive?"

Until that moment, I had forgotten about the money that the German soldier had given me.

"I have money," I said, pulling it out of my pocket.

"How did you get that?" Janusch cried.

I explained, and together we counted the notes. If we could find food to buy, it was enough to keep us alive. For a while at least.

"I have another idea," Janusch said. "We could try to get

out of the ghetto, and join the partisans. Someone I know can help us."

Adam looked at him, then at me.

"What choice do we have?" Janusch said. "We starve or get killed in the street. Or we're rounded up and taken off to Treblinka. Each of those choices means we die."

"Janusch is right," my brother said fiercely. "There's nothing here for us. Given we were going to die anyway, why not die fighting?"

Standing there, next to the bodies of the last of our family, what could I do but nod helplessly.

"Just tell me what to do."

The following morning I went to see Eva.

"Oh, Hanna!" she said, embracing me after hearing my news. "But are you really going to leave?"

"You are my only reason to stay here now. And I wanted to ask if you could come too?"

Eva looked at me. Then her eyes clouded over. "Do you still have that note from the book of Ruth I gave you?"

"Of course, always." I fished it out of my pocket and read, *"Where you go I will go, and where you stay I will stay."*

"I wish that were still my answer but I can't go with you. I can't leave poor Mama. Not now. And you can't stay."

"I don't know how to say goodbye to you." I said, my throat tightening.

"Then don't," she responded, kissing me gently on both cheeks as a silent farewell.

That night, Adam, Janusch and I went through our belongings, such as they were. I put on all the clothes I owned and some of Mama's. I put my tattered gymnastic ribbon and Eva's lucky silver rabbit in a pocket. They were the only things I wanted to take.

Adam carefully placed his violin on his bed and stood up to leave.

"You sure you don't want to take it with us?"

He nodded. "It's no use to me now."

"Best to travel light," Janusch said.

I took one last look at the rooms that had been our home for almost two years. They weren't much to look at, and any memories worth keeping I would carry with me. There were too many things I just wanted to forget.

We set off, using the same underground route through the cellars that Karol and his gang had used. Once outside the ghetto, Janusch led us through the streets. "Move fast, stay in the shadows, and don't look nervous," he warned us.

"Easier said," I muttered.

Within a few minutes we had entered a house and made our way down to the cellar.

Two young men were waiting to meet us.

They wore similar shabby clothes, their skin was sallow, and their faces unshaven. There was nothing about them that hinted they were Jews. No star on their clothes to identify them.

Janusch introduced us. "This is Pieter," he said, pointing to the taller one, "and this is Mariek."

We shared what little food we had as Pieter and Mariek explained that they belonged to Hashomer Hatzair, a Jewish youth group that had joined forces with the ZOB.

"Which is?" Adam asked.

"The Jewish Combat Organization," Mariek answered. "We've started working with the Home Army."

"We've all lost family and friends. Not many of us have anyone left," Pieter said. "But this isn't the time for us to mourn. Instead we must do what we can to stop them destroying us completely. Now it's time to fight back."

Janusch and Adam nodded in agreement.

"We're going to fight to our last breath, Mariek said vehemently. "We've got nothing left to lose."

Soon we were joined by two girls. One introduced herself as Sonia, the other as Sophie. I think they were both in their late teens. They wore men's clothes and caps and were treated like brothers.

They greeted us warmly. Sonia had brought me a pair of boy's trousers and some boots that didn't leak too badly.

"Do you know how to use a pistol?" Sophie asked me.

I shook my head.

"Don't worry, you'll learn quickly, I'm sure," Mariek said. "These girls are crack shots. They've taught me a thing or two," he added and laughed.

"Like what?" Adam asked.

"How to blow up a house. How to load a machine gun."

I was impressed.

"Shall we start now?" Sonia asked.

"Now? Learning to shoot?" I didn't realize we were to start training immediately.

"No?" Sonia threw her head back and smiled. "But there's a few tricks you can learn to defend yourself. Pieter, do you mind standing over here?" She motioned for Pieter to stand just in front of her. Quick as a wink, he was lying on the floor with Sonia's foot planted firmly on his chest.

"Again?" She smiled at Pieter. He stood up, grinning sheepishly. Sonia grabbed his arm and showed me how to twist behind him. She moved fast, and before I knew it, she had pushed Pieter face forward onto the floor.

"Do you want to try?"

"I'm a lot smaller than you," I said doubtfully, "but I'm game."

"It's technique, not size, that you need. Give it a go."

I copied every movement Sonia showed me, and to my amazement, Pieter was on the floor once again.

"Hey, you're pretty nimble," Mariek admitted.

"My sister did gymnastics for years." Adam's voice was full of pride.

That was the first time I had heard him praise my gymnastics. I'd always believed he thought it frivolous.

"Let's get some sleep," Sophie suggested. "And tomorrow we have a job for you to do."

I felt a huge urge of excitement. I hadn't felt anything like this since my performance in front of those German soldiers. I had been so miserable in the past few months I had forgotten the words that had sustained me those long months in the ghetto: *"Pluck and courage . . . pluck and audacity."* I repeated them over and over.

I settled into a corner of the cellar and slept more soundly than I had in years.

The next morning, Sophie gently shook me awake.

"C'mon," she said.

"You're to meet our commander, Mordechai Anielewicz, today." Pieter said. "And then we'll work out the best way you can help."

"You're all small, and that helps with smuggling," Mariek said. "There's a lot of ammunition needing to be moved."

"And with a bit more training, you'll be a force to be reckoned with." Sonia winked at me as she said this. "You especially. You've got fire in your eyes this morning."

It was true. I had woken up with a sense of purpose. I

couldn't wait to get going. After years of hiding, and persecution, I finally had a chance to do something positive. I had a chance to work with people with a common cause. I remembered Zaida's words: "In the end they can't win. The final triumph must always go to a just cause."

Adam leaned over and took my hand. "Do you remember when you told me the story of *The Scarlet Pimpernel*?"

"Of course I do. Why?"

"You told me that he worked with a band of friends, and together they worked to save others." He smiled. "Look around you."

I looked around, at Adam, Janusch, Sophie, Sonia, Pieter and Mariek, and smiled back. "Of course. We're part of a cause now. A just cause. One worth dying for." I held onto Adam's hand tightly.

"And one worth living for?"

I nodded.

After all, it is what we had promised.

# HISTORICAL NOTES

The Holocaust occurred during the Second World War when Hitler was leader of Germany. It is thought that the Nazis murdered as many as 17 million innocent people they considered "unworthy of life." This was a time of devastation, corruption and cruelty.

Adolf Hitler was an aspiring Austrian artist who had fought for Germany in the First World War. After Germany lost the war, it was left almost destitute. People were looking for someone to blame.

In the early 1920s Hitler became involved in German politics, and in 1923 his fledgling fascist party attempted a coup, known as the Beer Hall Putsch. It failed and Hitler was sent to jail for treason. There, he wrote down his political beliefs in a book he titled *Mein Kampf*, "My Struggle."

Hitler's beliefs were divisive and destructive. He believed that the Germans were a "master race," that he labelled "Aryans." He blamed the Jews for everything that had gone wrong, although this was completely untrue. He considered Jewish people, and also gypsies and others, to be less than human. He promised that when he became ruler of Germany he would rid the country of all Jews.

Hitler was released from prison on the eve of the Great Depression. The terrible poverty that was running rife in the country, and Hitler's gifts as a speaker, combined to convince the German people that they were a great race who had been wronged.

Hitler became Reich Chancellor of Germany in 1933, and Führer of Germany in 1934.

As soon as Hitler became Chancellor he began to make laws that removed rights from the Jewish population. Attacks were made on Jewish businesses and homes. On 9 November 1938 many Jewish homes and businesses were burnt down or vandalized. This night was called the *Kristallnacht* or "Night of Broken Glass."

Other countries, including Britain and France, were very unhappy about the direction that Germany was taking. There were diplomatic talks, but to no avail. In September 1939, Hitler invaded Poland.

From 1939 to 1940, the German army conquered much of northern Europe. When they took over a city, they forced all the Jews of that city into an area called a ghetto. These were fenced in with walls and barbed wire and heavily guarded. There was never enough food, water or medicine. Many families were forced to share a single room. But the Nazis' major aim was to place all Jews, plus all gypsies and any mentally and physically handicapped people, into concentration camps where they would die. Concentration camps were prison camps where people were forced to do hard labour. The weak were quickly killed or starved to death. Some concentration camps also had gas chambers. Large groups of people were led into these chambers and poisoned.

If families escaped being rounded up and were able to hide, they and their rescuers faced many challenges. They were forced to hide in cellars and attics where they had to keep quiet for hours on end. In rural areas, children lived in barns, chicken coops and forest huts. Any conversation or footsteps could start a police raid. During bombings, Jewish children had to remain hidden, unable to reach the safety of shelters. Under these conditions, the children were bored and frightened. Many children were killed.

Some children could pass as non-Jews. They had to carefully conceal their Jewish identity from neighbours, classmates, informers, blackmailers and the police.

Living as a non-Jew required false identity papers, which were often gained through contacts with the anti-Nazi resistance forces. Using these papers, Jews took on another name. But these papers were risky since Germans and police examined everyone's identity documents as they searched for Jews and resistance members.

Some Jewish children did survive because they were protected by kind people. Some Catholic convents in German-occupied Poland took in Jewish youngsters. Some Belgian Catholics hid children in their homes, schools and orphanages. Some French Protestant townspeople sheltered several thousand Jews. In Albania and Yugoslavia, some Muslim families concealed youngsters.

Children quickly learned to master the prayers and rituals of their "adopted" religion. Many Jewish youngsters were baptized into Christianity, mostly without their parents' knowledge.

Finding a rescuer was difficult, particularly one who would take care of his or her charges for a period of years. Some people took advantage of a persecuted family's desperation by demanding money, then reneging on their promise of aid. Or worse, turning them over to the authorities for bigger rewards. More commonly, stress, anguish and fear drove these benefactors to force Jewish children away from their homes.

Organized rescue groups frequently moved youngsters from one family or institution to another. In the German-occupied Netherlands, Jewish children stayed in an average of more than four different places; some changed hiding places more than a dozen times.

Among the most painful memories for hidden children was their separation from parents, grandparents and siblings. For a variety of reasons—lack of space, the inability or unwillingness of a rescuer to take in an entire family, or parents deciding not to abandon other family members in the ghetto—many Jewish children went into hiding alone. Separation tormented both parents and children. Each feared for the other's safety but they were powerless. For many hidden children, the wartime separation became permanent.

A hidden child's safety and security demanded strict secrecy. Foster families claimed the child was a distant relative, or a friend, or the surviving member of a bombed-out household. Convents and orphanages hid youngsters' Jewish identities. In some rescue networks, parents were not permitted to contact their children or know their whereabouts.

The children themselves understood the need for secrecy. They kept away from situations where their true identity might be exposed, held fast to their false names and religion, and avoided mannerisms or language that might be construed as Jewish or foreign. Jewish children who lived in hiding generally were treated well by their rescuers. But not always.

For Aryan-looking school-age children that were being hidden, the routines of going to class and studying helped to restore some sense of normality in their lives, and perhaps their new-made friends helped. Children who were physically concealed had few opportunities for formal study, but when possible, they too tried to educate themselves through reading and writing.

Life in hiding was always scary. German officials and their friends punished anyone who helped Jews, and offered rewards to anyone willing to turn them in. Beginning in March 1943, the Gestapo (the German secret state police) protected some Jews in Germany in exchange for tracking down Jews who had gone underground. By spring 1945, when the Nazi government fell, thousands of Jews had been turned in. In other countries, neighbours betrayed Jews in order to gain their money and property.

Following the defeat of Nazi Germany, the world learned of the staggering human toll of the Holocaust. Few Jewish children survived. In ghettos and concentration camps right across Europe, systematic murder, abuse, disease and medical experiments took many lives. Of the estimated 216,000 Jewish youngsters deported to Auschwitz Concentration Camp, only 6,700 teenagers were selected for forced labour. Nearly all the others died in the gas chambers. When the camp was liberated on 27 January 1945, Soviet troops found just 451 Jewish children among the 9,000 surviving prisoners.

In September 1939 approximately 1.6 million Jewish children were living in areas that the Germans or their allies would occupy. By the end of the war, at least 1.5 million Jewish children were dead. Soon after, Jewish agencies throughout Europe began tracing survivors and measuring losses. In the Low Countries—Belgium, the Netherlands and Luxembourg—only 9,000 Jewish children survived. Of the almost 1 million Jewish children living in 1939 Poland only about 5,000 survived, mostly by hiding.

Following the Holocaust, some Nazi party leaders were charged and convicted with crimes against humanity at the Nuremberg Trials.

Although justice was served in some cases, many

perpetrators of the Holocaust escaped prosecution. There could be no real restitution for the victims of the Holocaust. The crime was too great.

# GLOSSARY

**Aryan**

Hitler defined Aryans as Nordic Europeans, and called them the "master race." Nordic Europeans have fair skin and blue eyes. Hitler deemed other Caucasians to belong to Ayran sub-races. Other Europeans, such as the Slavs, including Russians and Serbians and ethnic Poles, were believed to be inferior and dangerous and fit for enslavement. Hitler described Jews and gypsies as the lowest of races and to be unworthy of life. Hitler's racist beliefs and doctrines were untrue and dangerous.

**Gestapo**

The Gestapo was Nazi Germany's feared secret police force. The Gestapo had its own courts and effectively acted as judge, jury and, frequently, executioner.

**Mensch**

Yiddish for "a person of integrity and honour."

**Nazi**

The Nazi Party was founded as the anti-semitic, or anti-Jewish, German Workers' Party in January 1919. By the early 1920s, Adolf Hitler had become leader and assumed all control. He renamed it the National Socialist German Workers' Party.

**Rosh Hashanah**

Jewish New Year and a time of celebration. The Jewish calender is based on cycles of the moon and dates back over five thousand years.

**SS (*Schutzstaffel*)**

Part of the German Nazi Party, they were a paramilitary organization whose methods of violent intimidation played a key role in Adolf Hitler's rise to power.

**Yom Kippur**

Jewish Day of Atonement when religious Jews fast and pray to God for forgiveness for the year's sins.

**Yiddish**

For nearly a thousand years, Yiddish was the primary language that Ashkenazi (European) Jews spoke. Unlike most languages, which are spoken by the residents of a particular area or by members of a particular nationality, Yiddish—at the height of its usage—was spoken by millions of Jews of different nationalities all over the globe.

**Warsaw Ghetto**

The Warsaw Ghetto was established in October 1940. The ghetto's walls were closed on November 1940. Over 400,000 Jews lived in the ghetto, an area of 3.4 km$^2$. The wall itself was built by Jews, under threat of death by Nazi soldiers. It was almost 3 metres (10 feet) high and topped with barbed wire and broken glass.

## ABOUT THE AUTHOR

Goldie Alexander's parents migrated from Poland to Australia just before the Second World War. Born in Melbourne, her first books for young adults were "Dolly Fiction" novels published under the pseudonym of Gerri Lapin. Her first book under her own name, *Mavis Road Medley*, is a time travel fiction exploring the world of Princes Hill and her parents' struggles to survive the Depression.

The author expresses thanks to Clare Hallifax for all her help and advice during the writing of this novel.